T0306286

50 World's Greatest Poems

CLASSICS

Reprint 2022

FINGERPRINT! CLASSICS
An imprint of Prakash Books India Pvt. Ltd.

113/A, Darya Ganj,
New Delhi-110 002
Tel: (011) 2324 7062 – 65, Fax: (011) 2324 6975
Email: info@prakashbooks.com/sales@prakashbooks.com

facebook www.facebook.com/fingerprintpublishing
twitter www.twitter.com/FingerprintP
www.fingerprintpublishing.com

ISBN: 978 93 8814 406 3

Processed & printed in India

Poetry is an art that is ever-evolving, its varying form, diction, and subjects from one century to another, bearing a proof to its mercurial temperament. Wordsworth and Coleridge, with the other Romantic poets, strove to compose poetry celebrating nature and imagination in simple words, consciously disengaging themselves from their earlier counterparts who strongly dictated that the purpose of poetry was didactic, and reason was always above imagination. In the meanwhile, the Court poets, such as Philip Sidney and Edmund Spenser, were content writing panegyrics for their patrons, and the Graveyard poets, such as Thomas Gray, spent their time musing on death.

Though divided into such schools, poetry has had common denominators notwithstanding the time it was written in. Love, war, religion, enemies, nature, objects, beauty, life, and even poetry and the life of the poet itself come under the umbrella of themes covered in verse.

This edition, carrying a wide range of fifty of the world's greatest poems, will allow you to immerse yourselves in the words composed by the father of English poetry as the Wife of Bath begins her lengthy Prologue to the tale, sing along with the groom as he calls for his bride in Spenser's *Epithalamion*, witness a possessive lover strangle his beloved in Browning's *Porphyria's Lover*, hear the repeated cries of 'Nevermore' of the raven in Edgar Allan Poe's poem, and much more. Explore the world of poetry from the fourteenth to the twentieth century in our eclectic collection of *50 World's Greatest Poems*.

CONTENTS

The Prologue to Wife of Bath's Tale (an excerpt)

by Geoffrey Chaucer

Published in

The Canterbury Tales

(1476)

*[*The Canterbury Tales *is a collection of twenty-four stories, but was supposed to have many more. Chaucer died in 1400, leaving his masterpiece incomplete. In the book, thirty pilgrims are travelling from London to Canterbury to visit St. Thomas Beckett's shrine. To pass the time, each of them has to tell two stories on their way, and two stories on their journey back.*

The Prologue is longer than the Wife of Bath's Tale. She is the only character in The Canterbury Tales *to have been given such a long prologue. Only the Pardoner's Prologue comes close to its length.]*

Experience, though none authority* *authoritative texts
Were in this world, is right enough for me
To speak of woe that is in marriage:
For, lordings, since I twelve year was of age,
(Thanked be God that *is etern on live),* *lives eternally*
Husbands at the church door have I had five,
For I so often have y-wedded be,
And all were worthy men in their degree.
But me was told, not longe time gone is
That sithen* Christe went never but ones *since
To wedding, in the Cane* of Galilee, *Cana
That by that ilk* example taught he me, *same

That I not wedded shoulde be but once.
Lo, hearken eke a sharp word for the nonce,*
*occasion
Beside a welle Jesus, God and man,
Spake in reproof of the Samaritan:
"Thou hast y-had five husbandes," said he;
"And thilke* man, that now hath wedded thee, *that
Is not thine husband:" thus said he certain;
What that he meant thereby, I cannot sayn.
But that I aske, why the fifthe man
Was not husband to the Samaritan?
How many might she have in marriage?
Yet heard I never tellen *in mine age* *in my life*
Upon this number definitioun.
Men may divine, and glosen* up and down;
*comment

But well I wot, express without a lie,
God bade us for to wax and multiply;[1]
That gentle text can I well understand.

---

1 The Wife of Bath extensively quotes the Bible to support her opinions in the prologue and tale. Here, she is justifying having five husbands, simply stating the she was obeying God who has asked man to increase and multiply.

Eke well I wot, he said, that mine husband
Should leave father and mother, and take to me;
But of no number mention made he,
Of bigamy or of octogamy;
Why then should men speak of it villainy?* *as if it
were a disgrace

Lo here, the wise king Dan* Solomon, *Lord
I trow that he had wives more than one;
As would to God it lawful were to me
To be refreshed half so oft as he!
What gift* of God had he for all his wives?
*special favour, licence
No man hath such, that in this world alive is.
God wot, this noble king, *as to my wit,* *as
I understand*
The first night had many a merry fit
With each of them, so *well was him on live.*
so well he lived
Blessed be God that I have wedded five!
Welcome the sixth whenever that he shall.
For since I will not keep me chaste in all,
When mine husband is from the world y-gone,

Some Christian man shall wedde me anon.[2]
For then th' apostle saith that I am free
To wed, *a' God's half,* where it liketh me.
on God's part
He saith, that to be wedded is no sin;
Better is to be wedded than to brin.* *burn
What recketh* me though folk say villainy**
*care **evil
Of shrewed* Lamech, and his bigamy?
*impious, wicked
I wot well Abraham was a holy man,
And Jacob eke, as far as ev'r I can.* *know
And each of them had wives more than two;
And many another holy man also.
Where can ye see, *in any manner age,*
in any period
That highe God defended* marriage *forbade
By word express? I pray you tell it me;

2 Critics have argued that the Wife of Bath's description of her husbands might have been coloured, and can't be taken for granted. She describes her first husband as 'goode', second one as 'riche', third one as 'olde', and the fourth as a 'reveler' and a two-timer. She launches into a long description of the fifth one since he was not the type of man that she would have considered to marry—he was young, poor, and difficult to dominate.

Or where commanded he virginity?
I wot as well as you, it is no dread,* *doubt
Th' apostle, when he spake of maidenhead,
He said, that precept thereof had he none:
Men may counsel a woman to be one,* *a maid
But counseling is no commandement;
He put it in our owen judgement.
For, hadde God commanded maidenhead,
Then had he damned* wedding out of dread;**
*condemned **doubt
And certes, if there were no seed y-sow,* *sown
Virginity then whereof should it grow?
Paul durste not commanden, at the least,
A thing of which his Master gave no hest.*
*command
The dart* is set up for virginity; *goal
Catch whoso may, who runneth best let see.
But this word is not ta'en of every wight,
But there as God will give it of his might.
except where
I wot well that th' apostle was a maid,
But natheless, although he wrote and said,
He would that every wight were such as he,
All is but counsel to virginity.
And, since to be a wife he gave me leave

Of indulgence, so is it no repreve*
*scandal, reproach
To wedde me, if that my make* should die,
*mate, husband
Without exception* of bigamy; *charge, reproach
All were it good no woman for to touch
though it might be
(He meant as in his bed or in his couch),
For peril is both fire and tow t'assemble
Ye know what this example may resemble.
This is all and some, he held virginity
More profit than wedding in frailty:
(*Frailty clepe I, but if* that he and she
*frailty I call it,
Would lead their lives all in chastity), unless*
I grant it well, I have of none envy
Who maidenhead prefer to bigamy;
It liketh them t' be clean in body and ghost;* *soul
Of mine estate* I will not make a boast. *condition

For, well ye know, a lord in his household
Hath not every vessel all of gold;
Some are of tree, and do their lord service.
God calleth folk to him in sundry wise,
And each one hath of God a proper gift,

Some this, some that, as liketh him to shift.*
*appoint, distribute
Virginity is great perfection,
And continence eke with devotion:
But Christ, that of perfection is the well,* *fountain
Bade not every wight he should go sell
All that he had, and give it to the poor,
And in such wise follow him and his lore:* *doctrine
He spake to them that would live perfectly, —
And, lordings, by your leave, that am not I;
I will bestow the flower of mine age
In th' acts and in the fruits of marriage.
Tell me also, to what conclusion* *end, purpose
Were members made of generation,
And of so perfect wise a wight* y-wrought? *being
Trust me right well, they were not made for nought.
Glose whoso will, and say both up and down,
That they were made for the purgatioun
Of urine, and of other thinges smale,
And eke to know a female from a male:
And for none other cause? say ye no?
Experience wot well it is not so.
So that the clerkes* be not with me wroth, *scholars
I say this, that they were made for both,
That is to say, *for office, and for ease* *for duty and

Of engendrure, there we God not displease.
for pleasure*
Why should men elles in their bookes set,
That man shall yield unto his wife her debt?
Now wherewith should he make his payement,
If he us'd not his silly instrument?
Then were they made upon a creature
To purge urine, and eke for engendrure.
But I say not that every wight is hold,* *obliged
That hath such harness* as I to you told, *equipment
To go and use them in engendrure;
Then should men take of chastity no cure.* *care
Christ was a maid, and shapen* as a man,
*fashioned
And many a saint, since that this world began,
Yet ever liv'd in perfect chastity.
I will not vie* with no virginity. *contend
Let them with bread of pured* wheat be fed, *purified
And let us wives eat our barley bread.
And yet with barley bread, Mark tell us can,
Our Lord Jesus refreshed many a man.
In such estate as God hath *cleped us,* *called us to
I'll persevere, I am not precious,* *over-dainty
In wifehood I will use mine instrument
As freely as my Maker hath it sent.

If I be dangerous* God give me sorrow; *sparing
    of my favours
Mine husband shall it have, both eve and morrow,
When that him list come forth and pay his debt.
A husband will I have, I *will no let,* *will bear
    no hindrance*
Which shall be both my debtor and my thrall,* *slave
And have his tribulation withal
Upon his flesh, while that I am his wife.
I have the power during all my life
Upon his proper body, and not he;[3]
Right thus th' apostle told it unto me,
And bade our husbands for to love us well;
All this sentence me liketh every deal.* *whit

---

3 To portray a fictional character of a woman who wanted complete power over her husband was something not seen in any work of Chaucer's time. In the Middle Ages, the time when *The Canterbury Tales* was published, women were considered inferior to men, so the husband was the one with power in a marriage.

Spring's Welcome

by John Lyly

Published in *Campaspe* (1584)

*[*Campaspe *was a play written by Lyly that centres around the beautiful Campaspe, who has been captured by Alexander, the legendary king of Macedonia.*

This poem is a song of one of the characters in the play—Trico, son to Sylvius, one of the citizens of Athens.]

What bird so sings, yet so does wail?
O 'tis the ravish'd nightingale.
Jug, jug, jug, jug, tereu! she cries,
And still her woes at midnight rise.
Brave prick-song! Who is't now we hear?
None but the lark so shrill and clear;
Now at heaven's gate she claps her wings,
The morn not waking till she sings.
Hark, hark, with what a pretty throat
Poor robin redbreast tunes his note!
Hark how the jolly cuckoos sing
Cuckoo! to welcome in the spring!
Cuckoo! to welcome in the spring!

Astrophil and Stella
(an excerpt)

by Philip Sidney

Published 1591

[Published five years after Philip Sidney's death, it narrates the love story of Astrophil and Stella in 108 sonnets and 11 songs.]

Loving in truth, and fain in verse my love to show,
That she,[1] dear she, might take some pleasure
of my pain,–
Pleasure might cause her read, reading
might make her know,
Knowledge might pity win, and pity grace obtain,–
I sought fit words to paint the blackest face of woe;
Studying inventions fine her wits to entertain,
Oft turning others' leaves, to see if thence would flow
Some fresh and fruitful showers upon my
sunburn'd brain.
But words came halting forth, wanting
invention's stay;
Invention, Nature's child, fled step-dame
Study's blows;
And others' feet still seem'd but strangers in my way.

---

1 Stella, Astrophil's beloved. Critics have observed how she has no voice in any of the sonnets, perhaps conforming with the courtly love tradition. Throughout the book, Stella is described only through Astrophil's gaze, and with the effects that she has on him. Also, Sidney was a courtier, and the poetry that courtiers circulated were supposed to portray ideal women—chaste, submissive, divine—who were loved platonically by men.

Thus great with child to speak and helpless
in my throes,
Biting my truant pen, beating myself for spite,
"Fool," said my Muse to me, "look in thy heart,
and write."

Epithalamion

by Edmund Spenser

Published in *Amoretti and Epithalamion* (1595)

[It is an ode to Spenser's bride-to-be, Elizabeth Boyle, written on 11 June 1594, their wedding day. She was his second wife.]

Ye learned sisters which have oftentimes
Beene to me ayding, others to adorne:
Whom ye thought worthy of your gracefull rymes,
That even the greatest did not greatly scorne
To heare theyr names sung in your simple layes,
But joyed in theyr prayse.
And when ye list your owne mishaps to mourne,
Which death, or love, or fortunes wreck did rayse,
Your string could soone to sadder tenor turne,
And teach the woods and waters to lament
Your dolefull dreriment.
Now lay those sorrowfull complaints aside,
And having all your heads with girland crownd,
Helpe me mine owne loves prayses to resound,
Ne let the same of any be envide:

So Orpheus did for his owne bride,[1]
So I unto my selfe alone will sing,
The woods shall to me answer and my Eccho ring.

Early before the worlds light giving lampe,
His golden beame upon the hils doth spred,
Having disperst the nights unchearefull dampe,
Doe ye awake, and with fresh lusty hed,
Go to the bowre of my beloved love,
My truest turtle dove,
Bid her awake; for Hymen[2] is awake,
And long since ready forth his maske to move,
With his bright Tead that flames with many a flake,

---

1 According to legend, Orpheus, son to King of Thrace and the muse, Calliope, played such beautiful melodies with his lyre that he enchanted not just humans, but also animals and beasts. On his beloved Eurydice's death, his sorrowful song moved even the Gods. Protected by them, he ventured into the Underworld, and played his lyre in front of the king, Hades (Pluto). Charmed, Hades informed Orpheus that he could have his beloved back. All he had to do was walk out of the Underworld playing his lyre, and not look back. Eurydice's shadow would follow him. But unable to hear his beloved's footsteps, Orpheus turned to look at her, steps away from the exit. As a result, Eurydice rescinded into the shadows, doomed to stay in the Underworld forever.

2 In Greek mythology, Hymen, or Hymenaeus, is a god of marriage, often invoked by writers of epithalamia to bless the wedding. In Greek art, he is depicted as a young, winged god, carrying a bridal torch.

And many a bachelor to waite on him,
In theyr fresh garments trim.
Bid her awake therefore and soone her dight,
For lo the wished day is come at last,
That shall for al the paynes and sorrowes past,
Pay to her usury of long delight:
And whylest she doth her dight,
Doe ye to her of joy and solace sing,
That all the woods may answer and your eccho ring.

Bring with you all the Nymphes that you can heare
Both of the rivers and the forrests greene:
And of the sea that neighbours to her neare,
Al with gay girlands goodly wel beseene.
And let them also with them bring in hand
Another gay girland
For my fayre love of lillyes and of roses,
Bound truelove wize with a blew silke riband.
And let them make great store of bridale poses,
And let them eeke bring store of other flowers
To deck the bridale bowers.
And let the ground whereas her foot shall tread,
For feare the stones her tender foot should wrong
Be strewed with fragrant flowers all along,
And diapred lyke the discolored mead.

Which done, doe at her chamber dore awayt,
For she will waken strayt,
The whiles doe ye this song unto her sing,
The woods shall to you answer and your Eccho ring.

Ye Nymphes of Mulla which with carefull heed,
The silver scaly trouts doe tend full well,
And greedy pikes which use therein to feed,
(Those trouts and pikes all others doo excell)
And ye likewise which keepe the rushy lake,
Where none doo fishes take,
Bynd up the locks the which hang scatterd light,
And in his waters which your mirror make,
Behold your faces as the christall bright,
That when you come whereas my love doth lie,
No blemish she may spie.
And eke ye lightfoot mayds which keepe the deere,
That on the hoary mountayne use to towre,
And the wylde wolves which seeke them to devoure,
With your steele darts doo chace from comming neer,
Be also present heere,
To helpe to decke her and to help to sing,
That all the woods may answer and your eccho ring.

Wake, now my love, awake; for it is time,
The Rosy Morne long since left Tithones bed,
All ready to her silver coche to clyme,
And Phoebus[3] gins to shew his glorious hed.
Hark how the cheerefull birds do chaunt theyr laies
And carroll of loves praise.
The merry Larke hir mattins sings aloft,
The thrush replyes, the Mavis descant playes,
The Ouzell shrills, the Ruddock warbles soft,
So goodly all agree with sweet consent,
To this dayes merriment.
Ah my deere love why doe ye sleepe thus long,
When meeter were that ye should now awake,
T'awayt the comming of your joyous make,
And hearken to the birds lovelearned song,
The deawy leaves among.
For they of joy and pleasance to you sing,
That all the woods them answer and theyr
eccho ring.

My love is now awake out of her dreames,
And her fayre eyes like stars that dimmed were

3 Also known as Apollo, the sun god, and god of music and poetry.

With darksome cloud, now shew theyr goodly
beames
More bright then Hesperus[4] his head doth rere.
Come now ye damzels, daughters of delight,
Helpe quickly her to dight,
But first come ye fayre houres which were begot
In Joves sweet paradice, of Day and Night,
Which doe the seasons of the yeare allot,
And al that ever in this world is fayre
Doe make and still repayre.
And ye three handmayds of the Cyprian Queene,
The which doe still adorne her beauties pride,
Helpe to addorne my beautifullest bride:
And as ye her array, still throw betweene
Some graces to be seene,
And as ye use to Venus, to her sing,
The whiles the woods shal answer and your
eccho ring.

Now is my love all ready forth to come,
Let all the virgins therefore well awayt,
And ye fresh boyes that tend upon her groome

---

4 The name given to Venus as the evening star.

Prepare your selves; for he is comming strayt.
Set all your things in seemely good aray
Fit for so joyfull day,
The joyfulst day that ever sunne did see.
Faire Sun, shew forth thy favourable ray,
And let thy lifull heat not fervent be
For feare of burning her sunshyny face,
Her beauty to disgrace.
O fayrest Phoebus, father of the Muse,
If ever I did honour thee aright,
Or sing the thing, that mote thy mind delight,
Doe not thy servants simple boone refuse,
But let this day let this one day be myne,
Let all the rest be thine.
Then I thy soverayne prayses loud will sing,
That all the woods shal answer and theyr eccho ring.

Harke how the Minstrels gin to shrill aloud
Their merry Musick that resounds from far,
The pipe, the tabor, and the trembling Croud,
That well agree withouten breach or jar.
But most of all the Damzels doe delite,
When they their tymbrels smyte,
And thereunto doe daunce and carrol sweet,
That all the sences they doe ravish quite,

The whyles the boyes run up and downe the street,
Crying aloud with strong confused noyce,
As if it were one voyce.
Hymen io Hymen, Hymen they do shout,
That even to the heavens theyr shouting shrill
Doth reach, and all the firmament doth fill,
To which the people standing all about,
As in approvance doe thereto applaud
And loud advaunce her laud,
And evermore they Hymen Hymen sing,
That al the woods them answer and theyr eccho ring.

Loe where she comes along with portly pace
Lyke Phoebe from her chamber of the East,
Arysing forth to run her mighty race,
Clad all in white, that seemes a virgin best.
So well it her beseemes that ye would weene
Some angell she had beene.
Her long loose yellow locks lyke golden wyre,
Sprinckled with perle, and perling flowres a tweene,
Doe lyke a golden mantle her attyre,
And being crowned with a girland greene,
Seeme lyke some mayden Queene.
Her modest eyes abashed to behold
So many gazers, as on her do stare,

Upon the lowly ground affixed are.
Ne dare lift up her countenance too bold,
But blush to heare her prayses sung so loud,
So farre from being proud.
Nathlesse doe ye still loud her prayses sing,
That all the woods may answer and your eccho ring.

Tell me ye merchants daughters did ye see
So fayre a creature in your towne before?
So sweet, so lovely, and so mild as she,
Adornd with beautyes grace and vertues store,
Her goodly eyes lyke Saphyres shining bright,
Her forehead yvory white,
Her cheekes lyke apples which the sun hath rudded,
Her lips lyke cherryes charming men to byte,
Her brest like to a bowle of creame uncrudded,
Her paps lyke lyllies budded,
Her snowie necke lyke to a marble towre,
And all her body like a pallace fayre,
Ascending uppe with many a stately stayre,
To honors seat and chastities sweet bowre.
Why stand ye still ye virgins in amaze,
Upon her so to gaze,
Whiles ye forget your former lay to sing,
To which the woods did answer and your eccho ring.

But if ye saw that which no eyes can see,
The inward beauty of her lively spright,
Garnisht with heavenly guifts of high degree,
Much more then would ye wonder at that sight,
And stand astonisht lyke to those which red
Medusaes[5] mazeful hed.
There dwels sweet love and constant chastity,
Unspotted fayth and comely womenhed,
Regard of honour and mild modesty,
There vertue raynes as Queene in royal throne,
And giveth lawes alone.
The which the base affections doe obay,
And yeeld theyr services unto her will,
Ne thought of thing uncomely ever may
Thereto approch to tempt her mind to ill.
Had ye once seene these her celestial threasures,

---

5 Medusa was one of the three Gorgon sisters. A priestess of Athena, she was a beautiful, golden-haired maiden, and had taken a vow of celibacy. The legend has multiple stories on how she became the infamous monster. One story goes that she had married Poseidon, thereby breaking her vow of being celibate, angering Athena. Another story describes that Poseidon had been pursuing Medusa relentlessly. Medusa had then sought refuge in the temple, hoping that Athena would protect her. Poseidon entered the temple and forced himself on her. The angry Athena punished her in both versions of the myth, turning every lock of hair on Medusa's head into a snake.

And unrevealed pleasures,
Then would ye wonder and her prayses sing,
That al the woods should answer and your
    eccho ring.

Open the temple gates unto my love,
Open them wide that she may enter in,
And all the postes adorne as doth behove,
And all the pillours deck with girlands trim,
For to recyve this Saynt with honour dew,
That commeth in to you.
With trembling steps and humble reverence,
She commeth in, before th'almighties vew:
Of her ye virgins learne obedience,
When so ye come into those holy places,
To humble your proud faces;
Bring her up to th'high altar that she may,
The sacred ceremonies there partake,
The which do endlesse matrimony make,
And let the roring Organs loudly play
The praises of the Lord in lively notes,
The whiles with hollow throates
The Choristers the joyous Antheme sing,
That al the woods may answere and their
    eccho ring.

Behold whiles she before the altar stands
Hearing the holy priest that to her speakes
And blesseth her with his two happy hands,
How the red roses flush up in her cheekes,
And the pure snow with goodly vermill stayne,
Like crimsin dyde in grayne,
That even th'Angels which continually,
About the sacred Altare doe remaine,
Forget their service and about her fly,
Ofte peeping in her face that seemes more fayre,
The more they on it stare.
But her sad eyes still fastened on the ground,
Are governed with goodly modesty,
That suffers not one looke to glaunce awry,
Which may let in a little thought unsownd.
Why blush ye love to give to me your hand,
The pledge of all our band?
Sing ye sweet Angels, Alleluya sing,
That all the woods may answere and your eccho ring.

Now al is done; bring home the bride againe,
Bring home the triumph of our victory,
Bring home with you the glory of her gaine,
With joyance bring her and with jollity.
Never had man more joyfull day then this,

Whom heaven would heape with blis.
Make feast therefore now all this live long day,
This day for ever to me holy is,
Poure out the wine without restraint or stay,
Poure not by cups, but by the belly full,
Poure out to all that wull,
And sprinkle all the postes and wals with wine,
That they may sweat, and drunken be withall.
Crowne ye God Bacchus with a coronall,
And Hymen also crowne with wreathes of vine,
And let the Graces daunce unto the rest;
For they can doo it best:
The whiles the maydens doe theyr carroll sing,
To which the woods shal answer and theyr
eccho ring.

Ring ye the bels, ye yong men of the towne,
And leave your wonted labors for this day:
This day is holy; doe ye write it downe,
That ye for ever it remember may.
This day the sunne is in his chiefest hight,
With Barnaby the bright,
From whence declining daily by degrees,
He somewhat loseth of his heat and light,
When once the Crab behind his back he sees.

But for this time it ill ordained was,
To chose the longest day in all the yeare,
And shortest night, when longest fitter weare:
Yet never day so long, but late would passe.
Ring ye the bels, to make it weare away,
And bonefiers make all day,
And daunce about them, and about them sing:
That all the woods may answer, and your eccho ring.

Ah when will this long weary day have end,
And lende me leave to come unto my love?
How slowly do the houres theyr numbers spend?
How slowly does sad Time his feathers move?
Hast thee O fayrest Planet to thy home
Within the Westerne fome:
Thy tyred steedes long since have need of rest.
Long though it be, at last I see it gloome,
And the bright evening star with golden creast
Appeare out of the East.
Fayre childe of beauty, glorious lampe of love
That all the host of heaven in rankes doost lead,
And guydest lovers through the nightes dread,
How chearefully thou lookest from above,
And seemst to laugh atweene thy twinkling light
As joying in the sight

Of these glad many which for joy doe sing,
That all the woods them answer and their echo ring.

Now ceasse ye damsels your delights forepast;
Enough is it, that all the day was youres:
Now day is doen, and night is nighing fast:
Now bring the Bryde into the brydall boures.
Now night is come, now soone her disaray,
And in her bed her lay;
Lay her in lillies and in violets,
And silken courteins over her display,
And odourd sheetes, and Arras coverlets.
Behold how goodly my faire love does ly
In proud humility;
Like unto Maia, when as Jove her tooke,
In Tempe, lying on the flowry gras,
Twixt sleepe and wake, after she weary was,
With bathing in the Acidalian brooke.
Now it is night, ye damsels may be gon,
And leave my love alone,
And leave likewise your former lay to sing:
The woods no more shal answere, nor your echo ring.

Now welcome night, thou night so long expected,
That long daies labour doest at last defray,

And all my cares, which cruell love collected,
Hast sumd in one, and cancelled for aye:
Spread thy broad wing over my love and me,
That no man may us see,
And in thy sable mantle us enwrap,
From feare of perrill and foule horror free.
Let no false treason seeke us to entrap,
Nor any dread disquiet once annoy
The safety of our joy:
But let the night be calme and quietsome,
Without tempestuous storms or sad afray:
Lyke as when Jove with fayre Alcmena lay,
When he begot the great Tirynthian groome:
Or lyke as when he with thy selfe did lie,
And begot Majesty.
And let the mayds and yongmen cease to sing:
Ne let the woods them answer, nor theyr eccho ring.

Let no lamenting cryes, nor dolefull teares,
Be heard all night within nor yet without:
Ne let false whispers, breeding hidden feares,
Breake gentle sleepe with misconceived dout.
Let no deluding dreames, nor dreadful sights
Make sudden sad affrights;
Ne let housefyres, nor lightnings helpelesse harmes,

Ne let the Pouke, nor other evill sprights,
Ne let mischivous witches with theyr charmes,
Ne let hob Goblins, names whose sence we see not,
Fray us with things that be not.
Let not the shriech Oule, nor the Storke be heard:
Nor the night Raven that still deadly yels,
Nor damned ghosts cald up with mighty spels,
Nor griesly vultures make us once affeard:
Ne let th'unpleasant Quyre of Frogs still croking
Make us to wish theyr choking.
Let none of these theyr drery accents sing;
Ne let the woods them answer, nor theyr eccho ring.

But let stil Silence trew night watches keepe,
That sacred peace may in assurance rayne,
And tymely sleep, when it is tyme to sleepe,
May poure his limbs forth on your pleasant playne,
The whiles an hundred little winged loves,
Like divers fethered doves,
Shall fly and flutter round about your bed,
And in the secret darke, that none reproves,
Their prety stelthes shal worke, and snares
shal spread
To filch away sweet snatches of delight,
Conceald through covert night.

Ye sonnes of Venus, play your sports at will,
For greedy pleasure, carelesse of your toyes,
Thinks more upon her paradise of joyes,
Then what ye do, albe it good or ill.
All night therefore attend your merry play,
For it will soone be day:
Now none doth hinder you, that say or sing,
Ne will the woods now answer, nor your Eccho ring.

Who is the same, which at my window peepes?
Or whose is that faire face, that shines so bright,
Is it not Cinthia, she that never sleepes,
But walkes about high heaven al the night?
O fayrest goddesse, do thou not envy
My love with me to spy:
For thou likewise didst love, though now unthought,
And for a fleece of woll, which privily,
The Latmian shephard once unto thee brought,
His pleasures with thee wrought.
Therefore to us be favorable now;
And sith of wemens labours thou hast charge,
And generation goodly dost enlarge,
Encline thy will t'effect our wishfull vow,
And the chast wombe informe with timely seed,
That may our comfort breed:

Till which we cease our hopefull hap to sing,
Ne let the woods us answere, nor our Eccho ring.

And thou great Juno, which with awful might
The lawes of wedlock still dost patronize,
And the religion of the faith first plight
With sacred rites hast taught to solemnize:
And eeke for comfort often called art
Of women in their smart,
Eternally bind thou this lovely band,
And all thy blessings unto us impart.
And thou glad Genius, in whose gentle hand,
The bridale bowre and geniall bed remaine,
Without blemish or staine,
And the sweet pleasures of theyr loves delight
With secret ayde doest succour and supply,
Till they bring forth the fruitfull progeny,
Send us the timely fruit of this same night.
And thou fayre Hebe, and thou Hymen free,
Grant that it may so be.
Til which we cease your further prayse to sing,
Ne any woods shal answer, nor your Eccho ring.

And ye high heavens, the temple of the gods,
In which a thousand torches flaming bright

Doe burne, that to us wretched earthly clods,
In dreadful darknesse lend desired light;
And all ye powers which in the same remayne,
More then we men can fayne,
Poure out your blessing on us plentiously,
And happy influence upon us raine,
That we may raise a large posterity,
Which from the earth, which they may long possesse,
With lasting happinesse,
Up to your haughty pallaces may mount,
And for the guerdon of theyr glorious merit
May heavenly tabernacles there inherit,
Of blessed Saints for to increase the count.
So let us rest, sweet love, in hope of this,
And cease till then our tymely joyes to sing,
The woods no more us answer, nor our eccho ring.

Song made in lieu of many ornaments,
With which my love should duly have bene dect,
Which cutting off through hasty accidents,
Ye would not stay your dew time to expect,
But promist both to recompens,
Be unto her a goodly ornament,
And for short time an endlesse moniment.

Shall I Compare Thee to a Summer's Day

by William Shakespeare

Published in

Shakespeare's Sonnets

(1609)

[One of the most well-known of the 154 sonnets that Shakespeare wrote.]

Shall I compare thee to a summer's day?[1]
Thou art more lovely and more temperate:
Rough winds do shake the darling buds of May,
And summer's lease hath all too short a date:
Sometime too hot the eye of heaven shines,
And often is his gold complexion dimm'd;
And every fair from fair sometime declines,
By chance, or nature's changing course, untrimm'd:
But thy eternal summer shall not fade,
Nor lose possession of that fair thou ow'st;
Nor shall Death brag thou wander'st in his shade,[2]
When in eternal lines to time thou grow'st:
    So long as men can breathe, or eyes can see,
    So long lives this, and this gives life to thee.

---

1 This sonnet is directed at a young man. Shakespeare dedicated the sonnets to a Mr. W. H. Over the years, people have tried to guess who this person was. Some believe it was William Herbert, Philip Sidney's nephew.

2 Not all readers hailed this as a love sonnet. One literary critic, James White Boyd said, 'This 'love poem' is actually written not in praise of the beloved, as it seems, but in praise of itself. Death shall not brag, says the poet; the poet shall brag. This famous sonnet is on this view one long exercise in self-glorification, not a love poem at all; surely not suitable for earnest recitation at a wedding or anniversary party, or in a Valentine.'

Death, Be Not Proud

by John Donne

Published in

Songs and Sonnets (1633)

Death, be not proud,[1] though some have called thee
Mighty and dreadful, for thou art not so;
For those whom thou think'st thou dost overthrow
Die not, poor Death, nor yet canst thou kill me.
From rest and sleep, which but thy pictures be,
Much pleasure; then from thee much more must flow,
And soonest our best men with thee do go,
Rest of their bones, and soul's delivery.
Thou art slave to fate,[2] chance, kings, and
    desperate men,
And dost with poison, war, and sickness dwell,
And poppy or charms can make us sleep as well
And better than thy stroke; why swell'st thou then?
One short sleep past, we wake eternally
And death shall be no more; Death, thou shalt die.[3]

---

1 According to John Carey in *John Donne: Life, Mind and Art* (1981), 'Death was an insult to his (Spenser) ego.' In this sonnet, Donne combats the terror of death by demystifying it, robbing it of its power and pride.

2 Personifyng death, arguing with it and calling it a slave to fate, such a feature is often termed as an extended metaphor known as a conceit, prominent in metaphysical poetry. Donne, known as a metaphysical poet, had garnered praise from many of his contemporaries. Samuel Johnson, while using the term 'metaphysical poets' in his *Lives of Poets*, ascribed it to writers 'recommended by the manner of Donne.'

3 This might have been inspired from the Bible—'The last enemy to be destroyed is death.'

Paradise Lost
(an excerpt)

by John Milton

Published 1667

He ended, and his words replete with guile
Into her heart too easy entrance won:
Fixed on the fruit she gazed, which to behold
Might tempt alone, and in her ears the sound
Yet rung of persuasive words, impregned
With reason, to her seeming, and with truth:
Meanwhile the hour of noon drew on, and waked
An eager appetite, raised by the smell
So savory of that fruit, which with desire,
Inclinable now grown to touch or taste,
Solicited her longing eye; yet first
Pausing awhile, thus to herself she mused.
"Great are thy virtues, doubtless, best of fruits,
Though kept from man, and worthy to be admired,
Whose taste, too long forborne, at first assay
Gave elocution to the mute, and taught
The tongue not made for speech to speak thy praise:
Thy praise he also who forbids thy use
Conceals not from us, naming thee the Tree
Of Knowledge,[1] knowledge both of good and evil;
Forbids us then to taste! but his forbidding

---

1 God had allowed Adam and Eve to enjoy everything in the garden, except eating from the Tree of Knowledge.

Commends thee more, while it infers the good
By thee communicated, and our want:
For good unknown sure is not had, or had
And yet unknown is as not had at all.
In plain then, what forbids he but to know,
Forbids us good, forbids us to be wise?
Such prohibitions bind not. But if death
Bind us with after-bands, what profits then
Our inward freedom? In the day we eat
Of this fair fruit, our doom is, we shall die.
How dies the serpent? he hath eaten and lives,[2]
And knows, and speaks, and reasons, and discerns,
Irrational till then. For us alone
Was death invented? or to us denied
This intellectual food, for beasts reserved?
For beasts it seems: yet that one beast which first
Hath tasted envies not, but brings with joy
The good befallen him, author unsuspect,
Friendly to man, far from deceit or guile.

---

2 Satan, disguising himself as a serpent, had cleverly argued that he had eaten the fruit, and it had given an animal like him an ability to speak. With this, he surmised that if an animal can become like him after eating the fruit, the benefits to a human must be immense. Satan had argued that perhaps God did not want Adam and Eve to eat from it since eating this fruit may bring their knowledge to God's level.

What fear I then? rather what know to fear
Under this ignorance of good and evil,
Of God or death, of law or penalty?
Here grows the cure of all, this fruit divine,
Fair to the eye, inviting to the taste,
Of virtue to make wise: what hinders then
To reach, and feed at once both body and mind?"

So saying, her rash hand in evil hour
Forth reaching to the fruit, she plucked, she eat:
Earth felt the wound, and Nature from her seat
Sighing through all her works gave signs of woe,
That all was lost. Back to the thicket slunk
The guilty serpent, and well might, for Eve
Intent now wholly on her taste nought else
Regarded, such delight till then, as seemed,
In fruit she never tasted, whether true
Or fancied so, through expectation high
Of knowledge: nor was Godhead from her thought.
Greedily she ingorged without restraint,
And knew not eating death.[3]

---

3 Adam, not wanting Eve to be doomed alone, eats the fruit. When God saw that they had disobeyed him, he banished them from the garden. So the death was not physical, but spiritual, of eternal separation of humankind from God.

To His Mistris Going to Bed

by John Donne

Published in 1669

Come, Madam, come, all rest my powers defie,
Until I labour, I in labour lie.
The foe oft-times having the foe in sight,
Is tir'd with standing though he never fight.
Off with that girdle, like heavens Zone glittering,
But a far fairer world incompassing.
Unpin that spangled breastplate which you wear,
That th'eyes of busie fooles may be stopt there.
Unlace your self, for that harmonious chyme,
Tells me from you, that now it is bed time.
Off with that happy busk, which I envie,
That still can be, and still can stand so nigh.
Your gown going off, such beautious state reveals,
As when from flowry meads th'hills shadow steales.
Off with that wyerie Coronet and shew
The haiery Diademe which on you doth grow:
Now off with those shooes, and then safely tread
In this loves hallow'd temple, this soft bed.
In such white robes, heaven's Angels us'd to be
Receavd by men; Thou Angel bringst with thee
A heaven like Mahomets Paradise; and though
Ill spirits walk in white, we easly know,
By this these Angels from an evil sprite,
Those set our hairs, but these our flesh upright.
Licence my roaving hands, and let them go,

Before, behind, between, above, below.
O my America! my new-found-land,
My kingdome, safliest when with one man man'd,
My Myne of precious stones, My Emperie,
How blest am I in this discovering thee!
To enter in these bonds, is to be free;
Then where my hand is set, my seal shall be.
  Full nakedness! All joyes are due to thee,
As souls unbodied, bodies uncloth'd must be,
To taste whole joyes. Gems which you women use
Are like Atlanta's balls, cast in mens views,
That when a fools eye lighteth on a Gem,
His earthly soul may covet theirs, not them.
Like pictures, or like books gay coverings made
For lay-men, are all women thus array'd;
Themselves are mystick books, which only wee
(Whom their imputed grace will dignifie)
Must see reveal'd. Then since that I may know;
As liberally, as to a Midwife, shew
Thy self: cast all, yea, this white lynnen hence,
There is no pennance due to innocence.
  To teach thee, I am naked first; why than
What needst thou have more covering then a man.

On Mr. Milton's Paradise Lost

by Andrew Marvell

Published 1674

[This poem was published in the second edition of Paradise Lost.*]*

When I beheld the poet blind,[1] yet bold,
In slender book his vast design unfold,
Messiah crowned, God's reconciled decree,
Rebelling Angels, the Forbidden Tree,
Heaven, Hell, Earth, Chaos, all; the argument
Held me a while, misdoubting his intent
That he would ruin (for I saw him strong)
The sacred truth to fable and old song,
(So Sampson groped the temple's posts in spite)
The world o'erwhelming to revenge his sight.

Yet as I read, soon growing less severe,
I liked his project, the success did fear;
Through that wide field how he his way should find
O'er which lame faith leads understanding blind;
Lest he perplexed the things he would explain,
And what was easy he should render vain.

---

1 Milton was completely blind by 1652. There have been only speculations on the cause of his blindness. That did not stop him from writing though and he went to compose a work of epic proportions—*Paradise Lost*.

Or if a work so infinite he spanned,
Jealous I was that some less skilful hand
(Such as disquiet always what is well,
And by ill imitating would excel)
Might hence presume the whole creation's day
To change in scenes, and show it in a play.
Pardon me, Mighty Poet, nor despise
My causeless, yet not impious, surmise.
But I am now convinced that none will dare
Within thy labors to pretend a share.
Thou hast not missed one thought that could be fit,
And all that was improper dost omit:
So that no room is here for writers left,
But to detect their ignorance or theft.
That majesty which through thy work doth reign
Draws the devout, deterring the profane.
And things divine thou treat'st of in such state
As them preserves, and thee, inviolate.
At once delight and horror on us seize,
Thou sing'st with so much gravity and ease;
And above human flight dost soar aloft,
With plume so strong, so equal, and so soft.
The bird named from that paradise you sing
So never flags, but always keeps on wing.

Where couldst thou words of such a compass find?
Whence furnish such a vast expanse of mind?
Just heaven thee, like Tiresias, to requite,
Rewards with prophecy the loss of sight.

Well mightst thou scorn thy readers to allure
With tinkling rhyme, of thine own sense secure;
While the Town-Bayes writes all the while and spells,
And like a pack-horse tires without his bells.
Their fancies like our bushy points appear,
The poets tag them; we for fashion wear.
I too, transported by the mode, offend,
And while I meant to praise thee must commend.
The verse created like thy theme sublime,
In number, weight, and measure, needs not rhyme.

Elegy Written in a Country Churchyard

by Thomas Gray

Published 1751

The curfew tolls the knell of parting day,
The lowing herd wind slowly o'er the lea,
The plowman homeward plods his weary way,
And leaves the world to darkness and to me.

Now fades the glimm'ring landscape on the sight,
And all the air a solemn stillness holds,
Save where the beetle wheels his droning flight,
And drowsy tinklings lull the distant folds;

Save that from yonder ivy-mantled tow'r
The moping owl does to the moon complain
Of such, as wand'ring near her secret bow'r,
Molest her ancient solitary reign.

Beneath those rugged elms, that yew-tree's shade,
Where heaves the turf in many a mould'ring heap,
Each in his narrow cell for ever laid,
The rude forefathers of the hamlet sleep.

The breezy call of incense-breathing Morn,
The swallow twitt'ring from the straw-built shed,
The cock's shrill clarion, or the echoing horn,
No more shall rouse them from their lowly bed.

For them no more the blazing hearth shall burn,
    Or busy housewife ply her evening care:
No children run to lisp their sire's return,
    Or climb his knees the envied kiss to share.

Oft did the harvest to their sickle yield,
    Their furrow oft the stubborn glebe has broke;
How jocund did they drive their team afield!
    How bow'd the woods beneath their sturdy stroke!

Let not Ambition mock their useful toil,
    Their homely joys, and destiny obscure;
Nor Grandeur hear with a disdainful smile
    The short and simple annals of the poor.

The boast of heraldry, the pomp of pow'r,
    And all that beauty, all that wealth e'er gave,
Awaits alike th' inevitable hour.
    The paths of glory lead but to the grave.

Nor you, ye proud, impute to these the fault,
    If Mem'ry o'er their tomb no trophies raise,
Where thro' the long-drawn aisle and fretted vault
    The pealing anthem swells the note of praise.

Can storied urn or animated bust
    Back to its mansion call the fleeting breath?
Can Honour's voice provoke the silent dust,
    Or Flatt'ry soothe the dull cold ear of Death?

Perhaps in this neglected spot is laid
    Some heart once pregnant with celestial fire;
Hands, that the rod of empire might have sway'd,
    Or wak'd to ecstasy the living lyre.

But Knowledge to their eyes her ample page
    Rich with the spoils of time did ne'er unroll;
Chill Penury repress'd their noble rage,
    And froze the genial current of the soul.

Full many a gem of purest ray serene,
    The dark unfathom'd caves of ocean bear:
Full many a flow'r is born to blush unseen,
    And waste its sweetness on the desert air.

Some village-Hampden, that with dauntless breast
    The little tyrant of his fields withstood;
Some mute inglorious Milton here may rest,
    Some Cromwell guiltless of his country's blood.

Th' applause of list'ning senates to command,
The threats of pain and ruin to despise,
To scatter plenty o'er a smiling land,
And read their hist'ry in a nation's eyes,

Their lot forbade: nor circumscrib'd alone
Their growing virtues, but their crimes confin'd;
Forbade to wade through slaughter to a throne,
And shut the gates of mercy on mankind,

The struggling pangs of conscious truth to hide,
To quench the blushes of ingenuous shame,
Or heap the shrine of Luxury and Pride
With incense kindled at the Muse's flame.

Far from the madding crowd's ignoble strife,
Their sober wishes never learn'd to stray;
Along the cool sequester'd vale of life
They kept the noiseless tenor of their way.

Yet ev'n these bones from insult to protect,
Some frail memorial still erected nigh,
With uncouth rhymes and shapeless sculpture deck'd,
Implores the passing tribute of a sigh.

Their name, their years, spelt by th' unletter'd muse,
The place of fame and elegy supply:
And many a holy text around she strews,
That teach the rustic moralist to die.

For who to dumb Forgetfulness a prey,
This pleasing anxious being e'er resign'd,
Left the warm precincts of the cheerful day,
Nor cast one longing, ling'ring look behind?

On some fond breast the parting soul relies,
Some pious drops the closing eye requires;
Ev'n from the tomb the voice of Nature cries,
Ev'n in our ashes live their wonted fires.

For thee, who mindful of th' unhonour'd Dead
Dost in these lines their artless tale relate;
If chance, by lonely contemplation led,
Some kindred spirit shall inquire thy fate,

Haply some hoary-headed swain may say,
"Oft have we seen him at the peep of dawn
Brushing with hasty steps the dews away
To meet the sun upon the upland lawn.

"There at the foot of yonder nodding beech
    That wreathes its old fantastic roots so high,
His listless length at noontide would he stretch,
    And pore upon the brook that babbles by.

"Hard by yon wood, now smiling as in scorn,
    Mutt'ring his wayward fancies he would rove,
Now drooping, woeful wan, like one forlorn,
    Or craz'd with care, or cross'd in hopeless love.

"One morn I miss'd him on the custom'd hill,
    Along the heath and near his fav'rite tree;
Another came; nor yet beside the rill,
    Nor up the lawn, nor at the wood was he;

"The next with dirges due in sad array
    Slow thro' the church-way path we saw him borne.
Approach and read (for thou canst read) the lay,
    Grav'd on the stone beneath yon aged thorn."

THE EPITAPH

Here rests his head upon the lap of Earth
    A youth to Fortune and to Fame unknown.
Fair Science frown'd not on his humble birth,
    And Melancholy mark'd him for her own.

Large was his bounty, and his soul sincere,
Heav'n did a recompense as largely send:
He gave to Mis'ry all he had, a tear,
He gain'd from Heav'n ('twas all he wish'd) a friend.

No farther seek his merits to disclose,
Or draw his frailties from their dread abode,
(There they alike in trembling hope repose)
The bosom of his Father and his God.

The Chimney Sweeper

by William Blake
Published in
Songs of Innocence (1789)

When my mother died I was very young,
And my father sold me while yet my tongue
Could scarcely cry " 'weep! 'weep! 'weep! 'weep!"[1]
So your chimneys I sweep & in soot I sleep.[2]

There's little Tom Dacre, who cried when his head
That curled like a lamb's back, was shaved,[3] so I said,
"Hush, Tom! never mind it, for when your head's bare,
You know that the soot cannot spoil your white hair."

And so he was quiet, & that very night,
As Tom was a-sleeping he had such a sight!
That thousands of sweepers, Dick, Joe, Ned, & Jack,
Were all of them locked up in coffins of black;

---

1 Chimney sweepers called out 'Sweep! Sweep!' to advertise their presence to their potential customers on the streets. Here, the child lisps 'weep', appallingly showing how incredibly young he was to be inducted into sweeping chimneys for a living.

2 The sweeper incharge of the day would pick a handful of children to clear the chimneys of ash and soot. Chimney sweeping was specifically assigned to children since they could easily fit inside the chimney. Most of them were orphans, though some were also sold into the trade by their parents for money, as in the case of the child in this poem.

3 The head was shaven to prevent their hair from catching fire while they swept the chimneys.

And by came an Angel who had a bright key,
And he opened the coffins & set them all free;
Then down a green plain, leaping, laughing they run,
And wash in a river and shine in the Sun.

Then naked & white, all their bags left behind,
They rise upon clouds, and sport in the wind.
And the Angel told Tom, if he'd be a good boy,
He'd have God for his father & never want joy.

And so Tom awoke; and we rose in the dark
And got with our bags & our brushes to work.
Though the morning was cold, Tom was happy
    & warm;
So if all do their duty, they need not fear harm.

A Poison Tree

by William Blake
Published in
Songs of Innocence and Experience (1794)

[The earlier title of the poem was 'Christian Forbearance'.]

I was angry with my friend;
I told my wrath, my wrath did end.
I was angry with my foe:
I told it not, my wrath did grow.

And I waterd it in fears,
Night & morning with my tears:
And I sunned it with smiles,
And with soft deceitful wiles.

And it grew both day and night.
Till it bore an apple bright.
And my foe beheld it shine,
And he knew that it was mine.

And into my garden stole,
When the night had veild the pole;
In the morning glad I see;
My foe outstretched beneath the tree.

A Red, Red Rose

by Robert Burns

Published 1794

O my Luve is like a red, red rose
    That's newly sprung in June;
O my Luve is like the melody
    That's sweetly played in tune.[1]

So fair art thou, my bonnie lass,
    So deep in luve am I;
And I will luve thee still, my dear,
    Till a' the seas gang dry.

Till a' the seas gang dry, my dear,
    And the rocks melt wi' the sun;
I will love thee still, my dear,
    While the sands o' life shall run.

And fare thee weel, my only luve!
    And fare thee weel awhile!
And I will come again, my luve,
    Though it were ten thousand mile.

---

1 According to *The Guardian*, when asked for the lyric or verse that has had the greatest impact on his life, the great American singer-songwriter, Bob Dylan quoted these lines from the poem.

The Rime of the Ancient Mariner

by Samuel Taylor Coleridge

Published in

Lyrical Ballads (1798)

[It is the longest poem that Coleridge ever wrote. Wordsworth had deemed the poem defective at first. There were plans to replace it if Lyrical Ballads *was reprinted. However, Wordsworth later acknowledged that the poem was passionate, had beautiful imagery, and a felicity of language.*

It was included in the reprint of Lyrical Ballads. *Coleridge reworked this poem for the reprints—removing archaic terms, simplifying the language, and adding a glossary.]*

Argument

How a Ship having passed the Line was driven by storms to the cold Country towards the South Pole; and how from thence she made her course to the tropical Latitude of the Great Pacific Ocean; and of the strange things that befell; and in what manner the Ancyent Marinere came back to his own Country.

PART I

It is an ancient Mariner,
And he stoppeth one of three.
'By thy long grey beard and glittering eye,
Now wherefore stopp'st thou me?

The Bridegroom's doors are opened wide,
And I am next of kin;
The guests are met, the feast is set:
May'st hear the merry din.'

He holds him with his skinny hand,
'There was a ship,' quoth he.
'Hold off! unhand me, grey-beard loon!'
Eftsoons his hand dropt he.

He holds him with his glittering eye—
The Wedding-Guest stood still,
And listens like a three years' child:
The Mariner hath his will.

The Wedding-Guest sat on a stone:
He cannot choose but hear;
And thus spake on that ancient man,
The bright-eyed Mariner.

'The ship was cheered, the harbour cleared,
Merrily did we drop
Below the kirk, below the hill,
Below the lighthouse top.

The Sun came up upon the left,
Out of the sea came he!
And he shone bright, and on the right
Went down into the sea.

Higher and higher every day,
Till over the mast at noon—'
The Wedding-Guest here beat his breast,
For he heard the loud bassoon.

The bride hath paced into the hall,
Red as a rose is she;
Nodding their heads before her goes
The merry minstrelsy.

The Wedding-Guest he beat his breast,
Yet he cannot choose but hear;
And thus spake on that ancient man,
The bright-eyed Mariner.

And now the STORM-BLAST came, and he
Was tyrannous and strong:
He struck with his o'ertaking wings,
And chased us south along.

With sloping masts and dipping prow,
As who pursued with yell and blow
Still treads the shadow of his foe,
And forward bends his head,
The ship drove fast, loud roared the blast,
And southward aye we fled.

And now there came both mist and snow,
And it grew wondrous cold:
And ice, mast-high, came floating by,
As green as emerald.

And through the drifts the snowy clifts
Did send a dismal sheen:
Nor shapes of men nor beasts we ken—
The ice was all between.

The ice was here, the ice was there,
The ice was all around:
It cracked and growled, and roared and howled,
Like noises in a swound!

At length did cross an Albatross,
Thorough the fog it came;
As if it had been a Christian soul,
We hailed it in God's name.

It ate the food it ne'er had eat,
And round and round it flew.
The ice did split with a thunder-fit;
The helmsman steered us through!

And a good south wind sprung up behind;
The Albatross did follow,
And every day, for food or play,
Came to the mariner's hollo!

In mist or cloud, on mast or shroud,
It perched for vespers nine;
Whiles all the night, through fog-smoke white,
Glimmered the white Moon-shine.'

'God save thee, ancient Mariner!
From the fiends, that plague thee thus!—
Why look'st thou so?'—With my cross-bow
I shot the ALBATROSS.[1]

---

1 The idea of killing the Albatross in the poem was given to Coleridge by William Wordsworth. On one of their walks, Coleridge, Wordsworth, and his sister, Dorothy, were discussing a book that Wordsworth had been reading—*Voyage Round the World by way of the Great South Sea*. In this book, Simon Hatley shoots an albatross, associating the bird with bad weather. For other crew members, it had been like a companion.

PART II

The Sun now rose upon the right:
Out of the sea came he,
Still hid in mist, and on the left
Went down into the sea.

And the good south wind still blew behind,
But no sweet bird did follow,
Nor any day for food or play
Came to the mariner's hollo!

And I had done a hellish thing,
And it would work 'em woe:
For all averred, I had killed the bird
That made the breeze to blow.
Ah wretch! said they, the bird to slay,
That made the breeze to blow!

Nor dim nor red, like God's own head,
The glorious Sun uprist:
Then all averred, I had killed the bird
That brought the fog and mist.

'Twas right, said they, such birds to slay,
That bring the fog and mist.

The fair breeze blew, the white foam flew,
The furrow followed free;
We were the first that ever burst
Into that silent sea.

Down dropt the breeze, the sails dropt down,
'Twas sad as sad could be;
And we did speak only to break
The silence of the sea!

All in a hot and copper sky,
The bloody Sun, at noon,
Right up above the mast did stand,
No bigger than the Moon.

Day after day, day after day,
We stuck, nor breath nor motion;
As idle as a painted ship
Upon a painted ocean.

Water, water, every where,
And all the boards did shrink;

Water, water, every where,
Nor any drop to drink.[2]

The very deep did rot: O Christ!
That ever this should be!
Yea, slimy things did crawl with legs
Upon the slimy sea.

About, about, in reel and rout
The death-fires danced at night;
The water, like a witch's oils,
Burnt green, and blue and white.
And some in dreams assurèd were
Of the Spirit that plagued us so;
Nine fathom deep he had followed us
From the land of mist and snow.[3]

---

2 One of the most quoted lines from the poem, which widely appears in popular culture, such as in the film *The Noah's Ark* (1999). A photo-animated visualization of the poem was made in 1975, directed by Raul da Silva. It also had a part explaining how Coleridge came to write the poem.

3 From here on, the poem enters into a fantastic, dream-like world. One of the interpretations of the supernatural elements that follow in the poem is that the mariner shot a harmless bird, a bird that symbolized nature itself. Making the mariner see horrific visions was nature's retaliation.

And every tongue, through utter drought,
Was withered at the root;
We could not speak, no more than if
We had been choked with soot.

Ah! well a-day! what evil looks
Had I from old and young!
Instead of the cross, the Albatross
About my neck was hung.

PART III

There passed a weary time. Each throat
Was parched, and glazed each eye.
A weary time! a weary time!
How glazed each weary eye,

When looking westward, I beheld
A something in the sky.

At first it seemed a little speck,
And then it seemed a mist;
It moved and moved, and took at last
A certain shape, I wist.

A speck, a mist, a shape, I wist!
And still it neared and neared:
As if it dodged a water-sprite,
It plunged and tacked and veered.

With throats unslaked, with black lips baked,
We could nor laugh nor wail;
Through utter drought all dumb we stood!
I bit my arm, I sucked the blood,
And cried, A sail! a sail!

With throats unslaked, with black lips baked,
Agape they heard me call:
Gramercy! they for joy did grin,
And all at once their breath drew in.
As they were drinking all.

See! see! (I cried) she tacks no more!
Hither to work us weal;
Without a breeze, without a tide,
She steadies with upright keel!

The western wave was all a-flame.
The day was well nigh done!
Almost upon the western wave

Rested the broad bright Sun;
When that strange shape drove suddenly
Betwixt us and the Sun.

And straight the Sun was flecked with bars,
(Heaven's Mother send us grace!)
As if through a dungeon-grate he peered
With broad and burning face.

Alas! (thought I, and my heart beat loud)
How fast she nears and nears!
Are those *her* sails that glance in the Sun,
Like restless gossameres?

Are those her *ribs* through which the Sun
Did peer, as through a grate?
And is that Woman all her crew?
Is that a DEATH? and are there two?
Is DEATH that woman's mate?

Her lips were red, *her* looks were free,
Her locks were yellow as gold:
Her skin was as white as leprosy,
The Night-mare LIFE-IN-DEATH was she,
Who thicks man's blood with cold.

The naked hulk alongside came,
And the twain were casting dice;
'The game is done! I've won! I've won!'
Quoth she, and whistles thrice.

The Sun's rim dips; the stars rush out;
At one stride comes the dark;
With far-heard whisper, o'er the sea,
Off shot the spectre-bark.

We listened and looked sideways up!
Fear at my heart, as at a cup,
My life-blood seemed to sip!
The stars were dim, and thick the night,
The steersman's face by his lamp gleamed white;
From the sails the dew did drip—
Till clomb above the eastern bar
The hornèd Moon, with one bright-star
Within the nether tip.

One after one, by the star-dogged Moon,
Too quick for groan or sigh,
Each turned his face with a ghastly pang,
And cursed me with his eye.

Four times fifty living men,
(And I heard nor sigh nor groan)
With heavy thump, a lifeless lump,
They dropped down one by one.

The souls did from their bodies fly,—
They fled to bliss or woe!
And every soul, it passed me by,
Like the whizz of my cross-bow!

PART IV

'I fear thee, ancient Mariner!
I fear thy skinny hand!
And thou art long, and lank, and brown,
As is the ribbed sea-sand.

I fear thee and thy glittering eye,
And thy skinny hand, so brown.'—
Fear not, fear not, thou Wedding-Guest!
This body dropt not down.

Alone, alone, all, all alone,
Alone on a wide wide sea!

And never a saint took pity on
My soul in agony.

The many men, so beautiful!
And they all dead did lie:
And a thousand thousand slimy things
Lived on; and so did I.

I looked upon the rotting sea,
And drew my eyes away;
I looked upon the rotting deck,
And there the dead men lay.

I looked to heaven, and tried to pray;
But or ever a prayer had gusht,
A wicked whisper came, and made
My heart as dry as dust.

I closed my lids, and kept them close,
And the balls like pulses beat;
For the sky and the sea, and the sea and the sky
Lay dead like a load on my weary eye,
And the dead were at my feet.

The cold sweat melted from their limbs,
Nor rot nor reek did they:
The look with which they looked on me
Had never passed away.

An orphan's curse would drag to hell
A spirit from on high;
But oh! more horrible than that
Is the curse in a dead man's eye!
Seven days, seven nights, I saw that curse,
And yet I could not die.

The moving Moon went up the sky,
And no where did abide:
Softly she was going up,
And a star or two beside—

Her beams bemocked the sultry main,
Like April hoar-frost spread;
But where the ship's huge shadow lay,
The charmèd water burnt alway
A still and awful red.

Beyond the shadow of the ship,
I watched the water-snakes:

They moved in tracks of shining white,
And when they reared, the elfish light
Fell off in hoary flakes.

Within the shadow of the ship
I watched their rich attire:
Blue, glossy green, and velvet black,
They coiled and swam; and every track
Was a flash of golden fire.

O happy living things! no tongue
Their beauty might declare:
A spring of love gushed from my heart,
And I blessed them unaware:
Sure my kind saint took pity on me,
And I blessed them unaware.

The self-same moment I could pray;
And from my neck so free
The Albatross fell off, and sank
Like lead into the sea.

PART V

Oh sleep! it is a gentle thing,
Beloved from pole to pole!
To Mary Queen the praise be given!
She sent the gentle sleep from Heaven,
That slid into my soul.

The silly buckets on the deck,
That had so long remained,
I dreamt that they were filled with dew;
And when I awoke, it rained.

My lips were wet, my throat was cold,
My garments all were dank;
Sure I had drunken in my dreams,
And still my body drank.

I moved, and could not feel my limbs:
I was so light—almost
I thought that I had died in sleep,
And was a blessed ghost.

And soon I heard a roaring wind:
It did not come anear;

But with its sound it shook the sails,
That were so thin and sere.

The upper air burst into life!
And a hundred fire-flags sheen,
To and fro they were hurried about!
And to and fro, and in and out,
The wan stars danced between.

And the coming wind did roar more loud,
And the sails did sigh like sedge,
And the rain poured down from one black cloud;
The Moon was at its edge.

The thick black cloud was cleft, and still
The Moon was at its side:
Like waters shot from some high crag,
The lightning fell with never a jag,
A river steep and wide.

The loud wind never reached the ship,
Yet now the ship moved on!
Beneath the lightning and the Moon
The dead men gave a groan.

They groaned, they stirred, they all uprose,
Nor spake, nor moved their eyes;
It had been strange, even in a dream,
To have seen those dead men rise.

The helmsman steered, the ship moved on;
Yet never a breeze up-blew;
The mariners all 'gan work the ropes,
Where they were wont to do;
They raised their limbs like lifeless tools—
We were a ghastly crew.

The body of my brother's son
Stood by me, knee to knee:
The body and I pulled at one rope,
But he said nought to me.

'I fear thee, ancient Mariner!'
Be calm, thou Wedding-Guest!
'Twas not those souls that fled in pain,
Which to their corses came again,
But a troop of spirits blest:

For when it dawned—they dropped their arms,
And clustered round the mast;

Sweet sounds rose slowly through their mouths,
And from their bodies passed.

Around, around, flew each sweet sound,
Then darted to the Sun;
Slowly the sounds came back again,
Now mixed, now one by one.

Sometimes a-dropping from the sky
I heard the sky-lark sing;
Sometimes all little birds that are,
How they seemed to fill the sea and air
With their sweet jargoning!

And now 'twas like all instruments,
Now like a lonely flute;
And now it is an angel's song,
That makes the heavens be mute.

It ceased; yet still the sails made on
A pleasant noise till noon,
A noise like of a hidden brook
In the leafy month of June,
That to the sleeping woods all night
Singeth a quiet tune.

Till noon we quietly sailed on,
Yet never a breeze did breathe:
Slowly and smoothly went the ship,
Moved onward from beneath.

Under the keel nine fathom deep,
From the land of mist and snow,
The spirit slid: and it was he
That made the ship to go.
The sails at noon left off their tune,
And the ship stood still also.

The Sun, right up above the mast,
Had fixed her to the ocean:
But in a minute she 'gan stir,
With a short uneasy motion—
Backwards and forwards half her length
With a short uneasy motion.

Then like a pawing horse let go,
She made a sudden bound:
It flung the blood into my head,
And I fell down in a swound.

How long in that same fit I lay,
I have not to declare;
But ere my living life returned,
I heard and in my soul discerned
Two voices in the air.

'Is it he?' quoth one, 'Is this the man?
By him who died on cross,
With his cruel bow he laid full low
The harmless Albatross.

The spirit who bideth by himself
In the land of mist and snow,
He loved the bird that loved the man
Who shot him with his bow.'

The other was a softer voice,
As soft as honey-dew:
Quoth he, 'The man hath penance done,
And penance more will do.'

PART VI

First Voice

'But tell me, tell me! speak again,
Thy soft response renewing—
What makes that ship drive on so fast?
What is the ocean doing?'

Second Voice

Still as a slave before his lord,
The ocean hath no blast;
His great bright eye most silently
Up to the Moon is cast—

If he may know which way to go;
For she guides him smooth or grim.
See, brother, see! how graciously
She looketh down on him.'

First Voice

'But why drives on that ship so fast,
Without or wave or wind?'

Second Voice

'The air is cut away before,
And closes from behind.

Fly, brother, fly! more high, more high!
Or we shall be belated:
For slow and slow that ship will go,
When the Mariner's trance is abated.'

I woke, and we were sailing on
As in a gentle weather:
'Twas night, calm night, the moon was high;
The dead men stood together.

All stood together on the deck,
For a charnel-dungeon fitter:
All fixed on me their stony eyes,
That in the Moon did glitter.

The pang, the curse, with which they died,
Had never passed away:
I could not draw my eyes from theirs,
Nor turn them up to pray.

And now this spell was snapt: once more
I viewed the ocean green,
And looked far forth, yet little saw
Of what had else been seen—

Like one, that on a lonesome road
Doth walk in fear and dread,
And having once turned round walks on,
And turns no more his head;
Because he knows, a frightful fiend
Doth close behind him tread.

But soon there breathed a wind on me,
Nor sound nor motion made:
Its path was not upon the sea,
In ripple or in shade.

It raised my hair, it fanned my cheek
Like a meadow-gale of spring—
It mingled strangely with my fears,
Yet it felt like a welcoming.

Swiftly, swiftly flew the ship,
Yet she sailed softly too:

Sweetly, sweetly blew the breeze—
On me alone it blew.

Oh! dream of joy! is this indeed
The light-house top I see?
Is this the hill? is this the kirk?
Is this mine own countree?

We drifted o'er the harbour-bar,
And I with sobs did pray—
O let me be awake, my God!
Or let me sleep alway.

The harbour-bay was clear as glass,
So smoothly it was strewn!
And on the bay the moonlight lay,
And the shadow of the Moon.

The rock shone bright, the kirk no less,
That stands above the rock:
The moonlight steeped in silentness
The steady weathercock.

And the bay was white with silent light,
Till rising from the same,

Full many shapes, that shadows were,
In crimson colours came.

A little distance from the prow
Those crimson shadows were:
I turned my eyes upon the deck—
Oh, Christ! what saw I there!

Each corse lay flat, lifeless and flat,
And, by the holy rood!
A man all light, a seraph-man,
On every corse there stood.

This seraph-band, each waved his hand:
It was a heavenly sight!
They stood as signals to the land,
Each one a lovely light;

This seraph-band, each waved his hand,
No voice did they impart—
No voice; but oh! the silence sank
Like music on my heart.

But soon I heard the dash of oars,
I heard the Pilot's cheer;

My head was turned perforce away
And I saw a boat appear.

The Pilot and the Pilot's boy,
I heard them coming fast:
Dear Lord in Heaven! it was a joy
The dead men could not blast.

I saw a third—I heard his voice:
It is the Hermit good!
He singeth loud his godly hymns
That he makes in the wood.
He'll shrieve my soul, he'll wash away
The Albatross's blood.

PART VII

This Hermit good lives in that wood
Which slopes down to the sea.
How loudly his sweet voice he rears!
He loves to talk with marineres
That come from a far countree.

He kneels at morn, and noon, and eve—
He hath a cushion plump:

It is the moss that wholly hides
The rotted old oak-stump.

The skiff-boat neared: I heard them talk,
'Why, this is strange, I trow!
Where are those lights so many and fair,
That signal made but now?'

'Strange, by my faith!' the Hermit said—
'And they answered not our cheer!
The planks looked warped! and see those sails,
How thin they are and sere!
I never saw aught like to them,
Unless perchance it were

Brown skeletons of leaves that lag
My forest-brook along;
When the ivy-tod is heavy with snow,
And the owlet whoops to the wolf below,
That eats the she-wolf's young.'

'Dear Lord! it hath a fiendish look—
(The Pilot made reply)
I am a-feared'—'Push on, push on!'
Said the Hermit cheerily.

The boat came closer to the ship,
But I nor spake nor stirred;
The boat came close beneath the ship,
And straight a sound was heard.

Under the water it rumbled on,
Still louder and more dread:
It reached the ship, it split the bay;
The ship went down like lead.

Stunned by that loud and dreadful sound,
Which sky and ocean smote,
Like one that hath been seven days drowned
My body lay afloat;
But swift as dreams, myself I found
Within the Pilot's boat.

Upon the whirl, where sank the ship,
The boat spun round and round;
And all was still, save that the hill
Was telling of the sound.

I moved my lips—the Pilot shrieked
And fell down in a fit;

The holy Hermit raised his eyes,
And prayed where he did sit.

I took the oars: the Pilot's boy,
Who now doth crazy go,
Laughed loud and long, and all the while
His eyes went to and fro.
'Ha! ha!' quoth he, 'full plain I see,
The Devil knows how to row.'

And now, all in my own countree,
I stood on the firm land!
The Hermit stepped forth from the boat,
And scarcely he could stand.

'O shrieve me, shrieve me, holy man!'
The Hermit crossed his brow.
'Say quick,' quoth he, 'I bid thee say—
What manner of man art thou?'

Forthwith this frame of mine was wrenched
With a woful agony,
Which forced me to begin my tale;
And then it left me free.

Since then, at an uncertain hour,
That agony returns:
And till my ghastly tale is told,
This heart within me burns.

I pass, like night, from land to land;
I have strange power of speech;
That moment that his face I see,
I know the man that must hear me:
To him my tale I teach.

What loud uproar bursts from that door!
The wedding-guests are there:
But in the garden-bower the bride
And bride-maids singing are:
And hark the little vesper bell,
Which biddeth me to prayer!

O Wedding-Guest! this soul hath been
Alone on a wide wide sea:
So lonely 'twas, that God himself
Scarce seemèd there to be.

O sweeter than the marriage-feast,
'Tis sweeter far to me,
To walk together to the kirk
With a goodly company!—

To walk together to the kirk,
And all together pray,
While each to his great Father bends,
Old men, and babes, and loving friends
And youths and maidens gay!

Farewell, farewell! but this I tell
To thee, thou Wedding-Guest!
He prayeth well, who loveth well
Both man and bird and beast.

He prayeth best, who loveth best
All things both great and small;
For the dear God who loveth us,
He made and loveth all.

The Mariner, whose eye is bright,
Whose beard with age is hoar,
Is gone: and now the Wedding-Guest
Turned from the bridegroom's door.

He went like one that hath been stunned,
And is of sense forlorn:
A sadder and a wiser man,
He rose the morrow morn.

Daffodils

by William Wordsworth

Published in *Poems in Two Volumes* (1807)

[On 15 April 1802, William Wordsworth and his sister Dorothy were walking around the shores of Ullswater, where they came across a field of daffodils. Dorothy described the beauty of the flowers in her journal, which inspired Wordsworth to write this poem.

Considered one of Wordsworth's best poems, at the time of its publication, the poem was not appreciated by Wordsworth's contemporaries. George Gordon Byron had criticized it for its 'puerile language'.]

I wandered lonely as a cloud
That floats on high o'er vales and hills,[1]
When all at once I saw a crowd,
A host, of golden daffodils;
Beside the lake, beneath the trees,
Fluttering and dancing in the breeze.

Continuous as the stars that shine
And twinkle on the milky way,
They stretched in never-ending line
Along the margin of a bay:

---

1 In Dorothy's journal entry for the day of the walk, she wrote how the daffodils 'tossed and reeled and danced, and seemed as if they verily laughed with the wind, that blew upon them over the lake.'

Ten thousand saw I at a glance,
Tossing their heads in sprightly dance.[2]

The waves beside them danced; but they
Out-did the sparkling waves in glee:
A poet could not but be gay,
In such a jocund company:
I gazed—and gazed—but little thought
What wealth the show to me had brought:

For oft, when on my couch I lie
In vacant or in pensive mood,
They flash upon that inward eye
Which is the bliss of solitude;
And then my heart with pleasure fills,
And dances with the daffodils.

---

2 Simplicity of language is one of the features of Romantic poetry. This poem is devoid of any words that might make it look fancier than prose. The aim was to write in a language that the common man would understand. Wordsworth, and the rest of the poets categorized as Romantics, increasingly insisted that they were different from their predecessors in the 18th century. They focused on imagination as opposed to reason, and proclaimed that poetic diction can be the same as prose.

Solitary Reaper

by William Wordsworth

Published in

Poems, in Two Volumes (1807)

Behold her, single in the field,
Yon solitary Highland Lass!
Reaping and singing by herself;
Stop here, or gently pass!
Alone she cuts, and binds the grain,
And sings a melancholy strain;[1]
O listen! for the Vale profound
Is overflowing with the sound.

No Nightingale did ever chaunt
So sweetly to reposing bands
Of Travellers in some shady haunt,
Among Arabian Sands:
No sweeter voice was ever heard
In spring-time from the Cuckoo-bird,
Breaking the silence of the seas
Among the farthest Hebrides.

---

1 A passage in Thomas Wilkinson's *Tours to the British Mountains*, is said to have inspired Wordsworth in constructing this reaper—'Passed a female who was reaping alone: she sung in Erse as she bended over her sickle; the sweetest human voice I ever heard: her strains were tenderly melancholy, and felt delicious, long after they were heard no more.'

Will no one tell me what she sings?
Perhaps the plaintive numbers flow
For old, unhappy, far-off things,
And battles long ago:
Or is it some more humble lay,
Familiar matter of to-day?
Some natural sorrow, loss, or pain,
That has been, and may be again!

Whate'er the theme, the Maiden sang
As if her song could have no ending;
I saw her singing at her work,
And o'er the sickle bending;—
I listened till I had my fill;
And, as I mounted up the hill,
The music in my heart I bore,
Long after it was heard no more.

Kubla Khan

by Samuel Taylor Coleridge

Published 1816

Or, a vision in a dream. A Fragment.

In Xanadu[1] did Kubla Khan
A stately pleasure-dome decree:
Where Alph, the sacred river, ran
Through caverns measureless to man
    Down to a sunless sea.
So twice five miles of fertile ground
With walls and towers were girdled round;
And there were gardens bright with sinuous rills,
Where blossomed many an incense-bearing tree;
And here were forests ancient as the hills,
Enfolding sunny spots of greenery.

But oh! that deep romantic chasm which slanted
Down the green hill athwart a cedarn cover!
A savage place! as holy and enchanted
As e'er beneath a waning moon was haunted
By woman wailing for her demon-lover!
And from this chasm, with ceaseless turmoil seething,
As if this earth in fast thick pants were breathing,
A mighty fountain momently was forced:

---

1 Xanadu was the palace of Kublai Khan, emperor of the Mongolian empire that his grandfather, Genghis Khan, had established. He rose to power in 1260.

Amid whose swift half-intermitted burst
Huge fragments vaulted like rebounding hail,
Or chaffy grain beneath the thresher's flail:
And mid these dancing rocks at once and ever
It flung up momently the sacred river.
Five miles meandering with a mazy motion
Through wood and dale the sacred river ran,
Then reached the caverns measureless to man,
And sank in tumult to a lifeless ocean;
And 'mid this tumult Kubla heard from far
Ancestral voices prophesying war!
    The shadow of the dome of pleasure
    Floated midway on the waves;
    Where was heard the mingled measure
    From the fountain and the caves.
It was a miracle of rare device,
A sunny pleasure-dome with caves of ice!

    A damsel with a dulcimer
    In a vision[2] once I saw:

---

2 The vision might be literal, since the poem is composed from the dream Coleridge saw one night, after he fell asleep reading this sentence in *Purchas' Pilgrimes*—'Here the Khan Kubla commanded a palace to be built, and a stately garden thereunto: and thus ten miles of fertile ground were enclosed with a wall.'

It was an Abyssinian maid
And on her dulcimer she played,
Singing of Mount Abora.
Could I revive within me
Her symphony and song,
To such a deep delight 'twould win me,
That with music loud and long,
I would build that dome in air,
That sunny dome! those caves of ice!
And all who heard should see them there,
And all should cry, Beware! Beware!
His flashing eyes, his floating hair!
Weave a circle round him thrice,
And close your eyes with holy dread
For he on honey-dew hath fed,
And drunk the milk of Paradise.

Hymn to Intellectual Beauty

by Percy Bysshe Shelley

Published in *Examiner* (1817)

The awful shadow of some unseen Power
    Floats though unseen among us; visiting
    This various world with as inconstant wing
As summer winds that creep from flower to flower;
Like moonbeams that behind some piny mountain
    shower,
        It visits with inconstant glance
        Each human heart and countenance;
Like hues and harmonies of evening,
        Like clouds in starlight widely spread,
        Like memory of music fled,
        Like aught that for its grace may be
Dear, and yet dearer for its mystery.

Spirit of BEAUTY, that dost consecrate
    With thine own hues all thou dost shine upon
    Of human thought or form, where art thou gone?
Why dost thou pass away and leave our state,
This dim vast vale of tears, vacant and desolate?
        Ask why the sunlight not for ever
        Weaves rainbows o'er yon mountain-river,[1]
Why aught should fail and fade that once is shown,

---

1 The imagery of the poem was inspired by the natural beauty of Lake Geneva. Shelley visited the lake with Byron in 1816.

Why fear and dream and death and birth
Cast on the daylight of this earth
Such gloom, why man has such a scope
For love and hate, despondency and hope?

No voice from some sublimer world hath ever
To sage or poet these responses given:
Therefore the names of Demon, Ghost, and Heaven,
Remain the records of their vain endeavour:
Frail spells whose utter'd charm might not avail to
sever,
From all we hear and all we see,
Doubt, chance and mutability.
Thy light alone like mist o'er mountains driven,
Or music by the night-wind sent
Through strings of some still instrument,
Or moonlight on a midnight stream,
Gives grace and truth to life's unquiet dream.

Love, Hope, and Self-esteem, like clouds depart
And come, for some uncertain moments lent.
Man were immortal and omnipotent,
Didst thou, unknown and awful as thou art,
Keep with thy glorious train firm state within his heart.
Thou messenger of sympathies,

That wax and wane in lovers' eyes;
Thou, that to human thought art nourishment,
Like darkness to a dying flame!
Depart not as thy shadow came,
Depart not—lest the grave should be,
Like life and fear, a dark reality.

While yet a boy I sought for ghosts, and sped
Through many a listening chamber, cave and ruin,
And starlight wood, with fearful steps pursuing
Hopes of high talk with the departed dead.
I call'd on poisonous names with which our youth
is fed;
I was not heard; I saw them not;
When musing deeply on the lot
Of life, at that sweet time when winds are wooing
All vital things that wake to bring
News of birds and blossoming,
Sudden, thy shadow fell on me;
I shriek'd, and clasp'd my hands in ecstasy!

I vow'd that I would dedicate my powers
To thee and thine: have I not kept the vow?
With beating heart and streaming eyes, even now
I call the phantoms of a thousand hours

Each from his voiceless grave: they have in vision'd
bowers
Of studious zeal or love's delight
Outwatch'd with me the envious night:
They know that never joy illum'd my brow
Unlink'd with hope that thou wouldst free
This world from its dark slavery,
That thou, O awful LOVELINESS,
Wouldst give whate'er these words cannot express.

The day becomes more solemn and serene
When noon is past; there is a harmony
In autumn, and a lustre in its sky,
Which through the summer is not heard or seen,
As if it could not be, as if it had not been!
Thus let thy power, which like the truth
Of nature on my passive youth
Descended, to my onward life supply
Its calm, to one who worships thee,
And every form containing thee,
Whom, SPIRIT fair, thy spells did bind
To fear himself, and love all human kind.

Don Juan
(an excerpt)

by George Gordon Byron

Canto II

Published 1819

[The poem is divided into sixteen cantos. The lines below have been taken from Canto II.]

Alas! they were so young, so beautiful,
So lonely, loving, helpless, and the hour
Was that in which the heart is always full,
And, having o'er itself no further power,
Prompts deeds eternity can not annul,
But pays off moments in an endless shower
Of hell-fire—all prepared for people giving
Pleasure or pain to one another living.

Alas! for Juan[1] and Haidee![2] they were
So loving and so lovely—till then never,
Excepting our first parents, such a pair

---

1 There are many versions of Don Juan's story, all of them depicting him as a womanizer. This character made his first appearance in *El Burlardor de Sevilla* (The Trickster of Seville), a tragic play. After seducing a woman, and killing her father, the commander of Seville, he mocked the statue of the commander, inviting it to join the feast. The statue came alive, pushing Juan into hell. In Byron's epic, Don Juan is only a naïve, young man who rather than seducing, gets seduced. Readers have even drawn parallels of Don Juan with Byron himself, who was infamous for being a philanderer.

2 Don Juan is washed ashore an island, where he is discovered by Haidee. They fall in love, but are eventually parted when her pirate father sells Juan into slavery.

Had run the risk of being damn'd for ever;
And Haidee, being devout as well as fair,
Had, doubtless, heard about the Stygian river,
And hell and purgatory—but forgot
Just in the very crisis she should not.

They look upon each other, and their eyes
Gleam in the moonlight; and her white arm clasps
Round Juan's head, and his around her lies
Half buried in the tresses which it grasps;
She sits upon his knee, and drinks his sighs,
He hers, until they end in broken gasps;
And thus they form a group that's quite antique,
Half naked, loving, natural, and Greek.

And when those deep and burning moments pass'd,
And Juan sunk to sleep within her arms,
She slept not, but all tenderly, though fast,
Sustain'd his head upon her bosom's charms;
And now and then her eye to heaven is cast,
And then on the pale cheek her breast now warms,
Pillow'd on her o'erflowing heart, which pants
With all it granted, and with all it grants.

Ode on a Grecian Urn

by John Keats

Published in *Annals of the Fine Arts* (1820)

Thou still unravish'd bride of quietness,
Thou foster-child of silence and slow time,
Sylvan historian, who canst thus express
A flowery tale more sweetly than our rhyme:
What leaf-fring'd legend haunts about thy shape
Of deities or mortals, or of both,
In Tempe or the dales of Arcady?
What men or gods are these? What maidens loth?
What mad pursuit? What struggle to escape?
What pipes and timbrels? What wild ecstasy?

Heard melodies are sweet, but those unheard
Are sweeter; therefore, ye soft pipes, play on;
Not to the sensual ear, but, more endear'd,
Pipe to the spirit ditties of no tone:
Fair youth, beneath the trees, thou canst not leave
Thy song, nor ever can those trees be bare;
Bold Lover, never, never canst thou kiss,
Though winning near the goal yet, do not grieve;
She cannot fade, though thou hast not thy bliss,
For ever wilt thou love, and she be fair!

Ah, happy, happy boughs! that cannot shed
Your leaves, nor ever bid the Spring adieu;
And, happy melodist, unwearied,

For ever piping songs for ever new;
More happy love! more happy, happy love!
For ever warm and still to be enjoy'd,
For ever panting, and for ever young;
All breathing human passion far above,
That leaves a heart high-sorrowful and cloy'd,
A burning forehead, and a parching tongue.

Who are these coming to the sacrifice?
To what green altar, O mysterious priest,
Lead'st thou that heifer lowing at the skies,
And all her silken flanks with garlands drest?
What little town by river or sea shore,
Or mountain-built with peaceful citadel,
Is emptied of this folk, this pious morn?
And, little town, thy streets for evermore
Will silent be; and not a soul to tell
Why thou art desolate, can e'er return.

O Attic shape! Fair attitude! with brede
Of marble men and maidens overwrought,
With forest branches and the trodden weed;
Thou, silent form, dost tease us out of thought
As doth eternity: Cold Pastoral!
When old age shall this generation waste,

Thou shalt remain, in midst of other woe
Than ours, a friend to man, to whom thou say'st,
"Beauty is truth, truth beauty,—that is all
Ye know on earth, and all ye need to know."

Ode to the West Wind

by Percy Bysshe Shelley

Published 1820

I.

O wild West Wind, thou breath of Autumn's being,
Thou, from whose unseen presence the
leaves dead
Are driven, like ghosts from an enchanter fleeing,[1]

Yellow, and black, and pale, and hectic red,
Pestilence-stricken multitudes: O thou,
Who chariotest to their dark wintry bed

The winged seeds, where they lie cold and low,
Each like a corpse within its grave, until
Thine azure sister of the Spring shall blow

Her clarion o'er the dreaming earth, and fill
(Driving sweet buds like flocks to feed in air)
With living hues and odours plain and hill:

---

1 Shelley explained in his notes to the poem that he had written the poem when he was in Florence. That day, the tempestuous wind had swept the Atlantic, bringing with it thunder and lightning.

Wild Spirit, which art moving everywhere;
Destroyer and preserver;[2] hear, oh hear!

II.

Thou on whose stream, mid the steep sky's commotion,
Loose clouds like earth's decaying leaves are shed,
Shook from the tangled boughs of Heaven and Ocean,

Angels of rain and lightning: there are spread
On the blue surface of thine aëry surge,
Like the bright hair uplifted from the head

Of some fierce Maenad, even from the dim verge
Of the horizon to the zenith's height,
The locks of the approaching storm. Thou dirge

Of the dying year, to which this closing night
Will be the dome of a vast sepulchre,
Vaulted with all thy congregated might

---

2 William Jones' and Edward Moore's *Hindu Pantheon* was known to Shelley, that spoke of the God, Shiva as both Destroyer and Preserver, which Shelley has applied to the West Wind.

Of vapours, from whose solid atmosphere
Black rain, and fire, and hail will burst: oh hear!

III.

Thou who didst waken from his summer[3] dreams
The blue Mediterranean, where he lay,
Lull'd by the coil of his crystalline streams,

Beside a pumice isle in Baiae's bay,
And saw in sleep old palaces and towers
Quivering within the wave's intenser day,

All overgrown with azure moss and flowers
So sweet, the sense faints picturing them! Thou
For whose path the Atlantic's level powers

Cleave themselves into chasms, while far below
The sea-blooms and the oozy woods which wear
The sapless foliage of the ocean, know

---

3 All seasons are mentioned in the poem, though winter is mentioned only in the line before the last, and there too the focus is on looking forward to the coming of spring.

Thy voice, and suddenly grow gray with fear,
And tremble and despoil themselves: oh hear!

IV.

If I were a dead leaf thou mightest bear;
If I were a swift cloud to fly with thee;
A wave to pant beneath thy power, and share

The impulse of thy strength, only less free
Than thou, O uncontrollable! If even
I were as in my boyhood, and could be

The comrade of thy wanderings over Heaven,
As then, when to outstrip thy skiey speed
Scarce seem'd a vision; I would ne'er have striven

As thus with thee in prayer in my sore need.
Oh, lift me as a wave, a leaf, a cloud!
I fall upon the thorns of life! I bleed!

A heavy weight of hours has chain'd and bow'd
One too like thee: tameless, and swift, and proud.

V.

Make me thy lyre, even as the forest is:
What if my leaves are falling like its own!
The tumult of thy mighty harmonies

Will take from both a deep, autumnal tone,
Sweet though in sadness. Be thou, Spirit fierce,[4]
My spirit! Be thou me, impetuous one!

Drive my dead thoughts over the universe
Like wither'd leaves to quicken a new birth!
And, by the incantation of this verse,

Scatter, as from an unextinguish'd hearth
Ashes and sparks, my words among mankind!
Be through my lips to unawaken'd earth

The trumpet of a prophecy! O Wind,
If Winter comes, can Spring be far behind?[5]

---

4 It is believed that Shelley wished to spread his revolutionary ideas through this poem. As opposed to being obedient to the tyrannical law, people, like the West Wind, should be 'wild' and 'tameless'. Shelley's revolutionary ideas troubled his life, starting from his days at the Oxford University. He had been rusticated for being the co-author of a controversial essay, *The Necessity of Atheism*.

5 Through this line, Shelley leaves no doubt in his reader's mind that change is inevitable, and so is a revolution.

To a Skylark

by Percy Bysshe Shelley

Published 1820

[On a summer evening in Livorno, Italy, Percy Bysshe Shelley was walking with his wife, Mary, when they both heard the caroling of a skylark. This inspired Shelley to compose the following poem.

It is often compared to William Wordsworth's poem of the same name.]

Hail to thee, blithe Spirit!
Bird thou never wert,
That from Heaven, or near it,
Pourest thy full heart
In profuse strains of unpremeditated art.

Higher still and higher
From the earth thou springest
Like a cloud of fire;
The blue deep thou wingest,
And singing still dost soar, and soaring ever singest.

In the golden lightning
Of the sunken sun,
O'er which clouds are bright'ning,
Thou dost float and run;
Like an unbodied joy whose race is just begun.

The pale purple even
Melts around thy flight;
Like a star of Heaven,
In the broad day-light
Thou art unseen, but yet I hear thy shrill delight,

Keen as are the arrows
Of that silver sphere,
Whose intense lamp narrows
In the white dawn clear
Until we hardly see, we feel that it is there.

All the earth and air
With thy voice is loud,
As, when night is bare,
From one lonely cloud
The moon rains out her beams, and Heaven is
overflow'd.

What thou art we know not;
What is most like thee?
From rainbow clouds there flow not
Drops so bright to see
As from thy presence showers a rain of melody.

Like a Poet hidden
In the light of thought,
Singing hymns unbidden,
Till the world is wrought
To sympathy with hopes and fears it heeded not:

Like a high-born maiden
In a palace-tower,
Soothing her love-laden
Soul in secret hour
With music sweet as love, which overflows her bower:

Like a glow-worm golden
In a dell of dew,
Scattering unbeholden
Its a{:e}real hue
Among the flowers and grass, which screen it from
the view:

Like a rose embower'd
In its own green leaves,
By warm winds deflower'd,
Till the scent it gives
Makes faint with too much sweet those heavy-winged
thieves:

Sound of vernal showers[1]
On the twinkling grass,
Rain-awaken'd flowers,
All that ever was
Joyous, and clear, and fresh, thy music
doth surpass.

Teach us, Sprite or Bird,[2]
What sweet thoughts are thine:
I have never heard
Praise of love or wine
That panted forth a flood of rapture so divine.

Chorus Hymeneal,
Or triumphal chant,
Match'd with thine would be all
But an empty vaunt,
A thing wherein we feel there is some hidden want.

---

1 W H Hudson once commented that a skylark's song was 'sunshine translated into sound.' *The Guardian* in its article 'The rare song of the skylark" states how the sound of the skylark 'has inspired more English poetry than any other birdsong except the nightingale's.'

2 The skylark is England's most common lark.

What objects are the fountains
Of thy happy strain?
What fields, or waves, or mountains?
What shapes of sky or plain?
What love of thine own kind? what ignorance of
    pain?

With thy clear keen joyance
Languor cannot be:
Shadow of annoyance
Never came near thee:
Thou lovest: but ne'er knew love's sad satiety.

Waking or asleep,
Thou of death must deem
Things more true and deep
Than we mortals dream,
Or how could thy notes flow in such a crystal stream?

We look before and after,
And pine for what is not:
Our sincerest laughter
With some pain is fraught;
Our sweetest songs are those that tell of
    saddest thought.

Yet if we could scorn
Hate, and pride, and fear;
If we were things born
Not to shed a tear,
I know not how thy joy we ever should come near.

Better than all measures
Of delightful sound,
Better than all treasures
That in books are found,
Thy skill to poet were, thou scorner of the ground!

Teach me half the gladness
That thy brain must know,
Such harmonious madness
From my lips would flow
The world should listen then, as I am listening now.

To Autumn

by John Keats

Published 1820

[This ode was the composed during the poet's walk to St. Giles, Winchester, in 1819.]

"Season of mists and mellow fruitfulness!
    Close bosom-friend of the maturing sun!
Conspiring with him how to load and bless[1]
    With fruit the vines that round the thatch-eaves
        run—
To bend with apples the mossed cottage trees,
    And fill all fruit with ripeness to the core—
To swell the gourd, and plump the hazel shells
    With a sweet kernel—to set budding, more
And still more, later flowers for the bees,
    Until they think warm days will never cease,
        For summer has o'er-brimmed their clammy
            cells.

Who hath not seen thee oft amid thy store?
    Sometimes whoever seeks abroad may find

---

1 Keats' allusion to conspiracy and loading weapons has not gone unnoticed, which led the readers to believe that this ode was not just about the beauty of a season but a veiled reference to Henry Hunt—the man who had been arrested for speaking at the Peterloo Massacre. Validating this sub-textual reading is the fact that Keats had penned a letter the day before composing this ode, to his brother and sister-in-law, describing Hunt's procession.

Thee sitting careless on a granary floor,
Thy hair soft-lifted by the winnowing wind;
Or on a half-reaped furrow sound asleep,
Drowsed with the fume of poppies, while thy hook
Spares the next swath and all its twinèd flowers;
And sometime like a gleaner thou dost keep
Steady thy laden head across a brook;
Or by a cider-press, with patient look,
Thou watchest the last oozings, hours by hours.

Where are the songs of Spring? Ay, where are they?
Think not of them—thou hast thy music too:
While barred clouds bloom the soft-dying day,
And touch the stubble-plains with rosy hue:
Then in a wailful choir the small gnats mourn
Among the river sallows, borne aloft
Or sinking, as the light wind lives or dies;
And full-grown lambs loud bleat from hilly bourn;
Hedge-crickets sing; and now with treble soft
The redbreast whistles from a garden-croft,
And gathering swallows twitter in the skies.

A Psalm of Life

by Henry Wadsworth Longfellow

Published in *The Knickerbocker* (1838)

What The Heart Of The Young Man Said To The Psalmist.

Tell me not, in mournful numbers,
    Life is but an empty dream![1]
For the soul is dead that slumbers,
    And things are not what they seem.

Life is real! Life is earnest!
    And the grave is not its goal;
Dust thou art, to dust returnest,
    Was not spoken of the soul.

Not enjoyment, and not sorrow,
    Is our destined end or way;
But to act, that each to-morrow
    Find us farther than to-day.

Art is long, and Time is fleeting,
    And our hearts, though stout and brave,

---

1 Eric S Robertson in *The Life of Henry Wadsworth Longfellow* wrote that this poem 'proclaims the gladness of living to be the best of poetry. It is not the best of poetry, but it makes the best theme for a preacher.' He also mentions that the poem was being talked about amongst the preachers and sung as a hymn in churches.

Still, like muffled drums, are beating
    Funeral marches to the grave.

In the world's broad field of battle,
    In the bivouac of Life,
Be not like dumb, driven cattle!
    Be a hero in the strife!

Trust no Future, howe'er pleasant!
    Let the dead Past bury its dead!
Act,— act in the living Present!
    Heart within, and God o'erhead!

Lives of great men all remind us
    We can make our lives sublime,
And, departing, leave behind us
    Footprints on the sands of time;

Footprints, that perhaps another,
    Sailing o'er life's solemn main,
A forlorn and shipwrecked brother,
    Seeing, shall take heart again.

Let us, then, be up and doing,
With a heart for any fate;
Still achieving, still pursuing,
Learn to labor and to wait.

My Last Duchess

by Robert Browning

Published in

Dramatic Lyrics (1842)

That's my last Duchess[1] painted on the wall,
Looking as if she were alive. I call
That piece a wonder, now; Fra Pandolf's hands
Worked busily a day, and there she stands.
Will't please you sit and look at her? I said
"Fra Pandolf" by design, for never read
Strangers like you that pictured countenance,
The depth and passion of its earnest glance,
But to myself they turned (since none puts by
The curtain I have drawn for you, but I)
And seemed as they would ask me, if they durst,
How such a glance came there; so, not the first
Are you to turn and ask thus. Sir, 'twas not
Her husband's presence only, called that spot
Of joy into the Duchess' cheek; perhaps
Fra Pandolf chanced to say, "Her mantle laps
Over my lady's wrist too much," or "Paint
Must never hope to reproduce the faint
Half-flush that dies along her throat." Such stuff
Was courtesy, she thought, and cause enough

---

1 The Duke of Ferrara most likely inspired the speaker of this poem. Browning had been reviewing a book on Tasso's life, in which he read an account of Alfonso II, the fifth duke of Ferrara, who had married the fourteen-year-old daughter of Cosimo de Medici, Lucrezia.

For calling up that spot of joy. She had
A heart—how shall I say?— too soon made glad,
Too easily impressed; she liked whate'er
She looked on, and her looks went everywhere.
Sir, 'twas all one! My favour at her breast,
The dropping of the daylight in the West,
The bough of cherries some officious fool
Broke in the orchard for her, the white mule
She rode with round the terrace—all and each
Would draw from her alike the approving speech,
Or blush, at least. She thanked men—good!
    but thanked
Somehow—I know not how—as if she ranked
My gift of a nine-hundred-years-old name
With anybody's gift. Who'd stoop to blame
This sort of trifling? Even had you skill
In speech—which I have not—to make your will
Quite clear to such an one, and say, "Just this
Or that in you disgusts me; here you miss,
Or there exceed the mark"—and if she let
Herself be lessoned so, nor plainly set
Her wits to yours, forsooth, and made excuse—
E'en then would be some stooping; and I choose
Never to stoop. Oh, sir, she smiled, no doubt,
Whene'er I passed her; but who passed without

Much the same smile? This grew; I gave commands;
Then all smiles stopped together.[2] There she stands
As if alive. Will't please you rise? We'll meet
The company below, then. I repeat,
The Count your master's known munificence
Is ample warrant that no just pretense
Of mine for dowry[3] will be disallowed;
Though his fair daughter's self, as I avowed
At starting, is my object. Nay, we'll go
Together down, sir. Notice Neptune, though,
Taming a sea-horse, thought a rarity,
Which Claus of Innsbruck cast in bronze for me!

---

2 Browning's poem is a dramatic monologue, giving an insight in the psychology of the only speaker of the poem—a possessive man who got his wife killed. Though his control over her does not stop even after her death, since he is the only one who can draw the curtain to show the painting.

3 The Count is being shown the painting of the Duke's former wife, since he is planning to marry the Count's daughter. The painting will serve as a warning to what will happen to her if she is ever disobedient.

Porphyria's Lover

by Robert Browning

Published in

Dramatic Lyrics (1842)

The rain set early in to-night,
The sullen wind was soon awake,
It tore the elm-tops down for spite,
And did its worst to vex the lake:
I listened with heart fit to break.
When glided in Porphyria; straight
She shut the cold out and the storm,
And kneeled and made the cheerless grate
Blaze up, and all the cottage warm;
Which done, she rose, and from her form
Withdrew the dripping cloak and shawl,
And laid her soiled gloves by, untied
Her hat and let the damp hair fall,
And, last, she sat down by my side
And called me. When no voice replied,
She put my arm about her waist,
And made her smooth white shoulder bare,
And all her yellow hair displaced,
And, stooping, made my cheek lie there,
And spread, o'er all, her yellow hair,
Murmuring how she loved me — she
Too weak, for all her heart's endeavour,
To set its struggling passion free
From pride, and vainer ties dissever,
And give herself to me for ever.

But passion sometimes would prevail,
    Nor could to-night's gay feast restrain
A sudden thought of one so pale
    For love of her, and all in vain:
    So, she was come through wind and rain.
Be sure I looked up at her eyes
    Happy and proud; at last I knew
Porphyria worshipped me; surprise
    Made my heart swell, and still it grew
    While I debated what to do.
That moment she was mine, mine, fair,
    Perfectly pure and good: I found
A thing to do, and all her hair
    In one long yellow string I wound
    Three times her little throat around,
And strangled her. No pain felt she;
    I am quite sure she felt no pain.[1]
As a shut bud that holds a bee,
    I warily oped her lids: again
    Laughed the blue eyes without a stain.

---

1 The way the speaker insists that Porphyria felt no pain, has been cited to claim that the speaker was not only obsessive, but a madman. Though people have also countered this view, saying that the lines are spoken by the man to simply reassure himself that he did right by killing her, to suppress his guilt.

And I untightened next the tress
    About her neck; her cheek once more
Blushed bright beneath my burning kiss:
    I propped her head up as before,
    Only, this time my shoulder bore
Her head, which droops upon it still:
    The smiling rosy little head,
So glad it has its utmost will,[2]
    That all it scorned at once is fled,
    And I, its love, am gained instead!
Porphyria's love: she guessed not how
    Her darling one wish would be heard.
And thus we sit together now,
    And all night long we have not stirred,
    And yet God has not said a word![3]

---

2 Porphyria is now dead and the readers have no way of knowing whether to die was her own will. Like the dramatic monologue in Browning's *My Last Duchess*, the point of view of the speaker is being projected as the woman's.

3 The speaker is using this as proof that he did nothing wrong in killing Porphyria. God, through his silence, is indicating that he condones this act.

Ulysses

by Alfred Tennyson

Published in *Poetry* (1842)

[The poem was composed by Tennyson soon after his friend, Arthur Henry Hallam's death. According to his memoirs, the poem is 'about the need of going forward, and braving the struggle of life.']

It little profits that an idle king,
By this still hearth, among these barren crags,
Match'd with an aged wife,[1] I mete and dole
Unequal laws unto a savage race,
That hoard, and sleep, and feed, and know not me.
I cannot rest from travel: I will drink
Life to the lees: All times I have enjoy'd
Greatly, have suffer'd greatly, both with those
That loved me, and alone, on shore, and when
Thro' scudding drifts the rainy Hyades
Vext the dim sea: I am become a name;
For always roaming with a hungry heart
Much have I seen and known; cities of men
And manners, climates, councils, governments,

---

1 Ulysses was the king of Ithaca, also known as Odysseus. In Homer's *Odyssey*, it is recounted that he had left his wife Penelope right after their marriage and returned twenty years later, shooting his wife's suitors as they were having an archery contest to decide who she will marry. He is the man who comes up with the subterfuge of using a wooden horse to smuggle Greek forces inside the city of Troy.

Myself not least, but honour'd of them all;
And drunk delight of battle with my peers,
Far on the ringing plains of windy Troy.
I am a part of all that I have met;
Yet all experience is an arch wherethro'
Gleams that untravell'd world whose margin fades
For ever and forever when I move.
How dull it is to pause, to make an end,
To rust unburnish'd, not to shine in use!
As tho' to breathe were life! Life piled on life
Were all too little, and of one to me
Little remains: but every hour is saved
From that eternal silence, something more,
A bringer of new things; and vile it were
For some three suns to store and hoard myself,
And this gray spirit yearning in desire
To follow knowledge like a sinking star,
Beyond the utmost bound of human thought.

This is my son, mine own Telemachus,
To whom I leave the sceptre and the isle,—
Well-loved of me, discerning to fulfil
This labour, by slow prudence to make mild
A rugged people, and thro' soft degrees
Subdue them to the useful and the good.

Most blameless is he, centred in the sphere
Of common duties, decent not to fail
In offices of tenderness, and pay
Meet adoration to my household gods,
When I am gone. He works his work, I mine.

There lies the port; the vessel puffs her sail:
There gloom the dark, broad seas. My mariners,
Souls that have toil'd, and wrought, and thought
with me—
That ever with a frolic welcome took
The thunder and the sunshine, and opposed
Free hearts, free foreheads—you and I are old;
Old age hath yet his honour and his toil;
Death closes all: but something ere the end,
Some work of noble note, may yet be done,
Not unbecoming men that strove with Gods.
The lights begin to twinkle from the rocks:
The long day wanes: the slow moon climbs: the deep
Moans round with many voices. Come, my friends,
'T is not too late to seek a newer world.[2]
Push off, and sitting well in order smite

---

2 This line has been taken as Tennyson's celebration of Victorian imperialism.

The sounding furrows; for my purpose holds
To sail beyond the sunset, and the baths
Of all the western stars, until I die.
It may be that the gulfs will wash us down:
It may be we shall touch the Happy Isles,
And see the great Achilles,[3] whom we knew.
Tho' much is taken, much abides; and tho'
We are not now that strength which in old days
Moved earth and heaven, that which we are, we are;
One equal temper of heroic hearts,
Made weak by time and fate, but strong in will
To strive, to seek, to find, and not to yield.[4]

---

3 Achilles was considered one of the bravest warriors of the Trojan War. Seemingly undefeatable, his only weak point was his heel. His mother, Thetis, the sea nymph dipped him in the river, Styx. His body was now indestructible, except for the heel, by which Thetis held him. Though Homer's Iliad doesn't mention his death, the poet Arctinus in Aetheopis wrote that Achilles is slain in battle by Paris' arrow.

4 The lines echo Satan's lines in *Paradise Lost*—
'All is not lost; the unconquerable will,
And study of revenge, immortal hate,
And courage never to submit or yield,
And what is else not to overcome?'

The Day Is Done

by Henry Wadsworth Longfellow

Published 1844

The day is done, and the darkness
    Falls from the wings of Night,
As a feather is wafted downward
    From an eagle in his flight.

I see the lights of the village
    Gleam through the rain and the mist,
And a feeling of sadness comes o'er me
    That my soul cannot resist:

A feeling of sadness and longing,
    That is not akin to pain,
And resembles sorrow only
    As the mist resembles the rain.

Come, read to me some poem,
    Some simple and heartfelt lay,
That shall soothe this restless feeling,
    And banish the thoughts of day.[1]

---

1 Henry Wardsworth Longfellow came to be known as a Fireside Poet, along with Oliver Wendell Holmes, and John Greenleaf Whittier. It was common for people in the nineteenth century to read from novels or poetry books, gathered around a fire with their friends and acquaintances. Here too, the speaker wishes to read a simple poem that may reduce his restlessness at the end of the day.

Not from the grand old masters,
Not from the bards sublime,
Whose distant footsteps echo
Through the corridors of Time.

For, like strains of martial music,
Their mighty thoughts suggest
Life's endless toil and endeavor;
And to-night I long for rest.

Read from some humbler poet,
Whose songs gushed from his heart,
As showers from the clouds of summer,
Or tears from the eyelids start;

Who, through long days of labor,
And nights devoid of ease,
Still heard in his soul the music
Of wonderful melodies.

Such songs have power to quiet
The restless pulse of care,
And come like the benediction
That follows after prayer.

Then read from the treasured volume
The poem of thy choice,
And lend to the rhyme of the poet
The beauty of thy voice.

And the night shall be filled with music,
And the cares, that infest the day,
Shall fold their tents, like the Arabs,
And as silently steal away.

The Raven

by Edgar Allan Poe

Published in

The Evening Mirror (1845)

[Poe had read Charles Dickens' Barnaby Rudge, *in which the protagonist is accompanied by a talking raven, named Grip. This raven supposedly inspired the following poem. It fetched him no more than five dollars when he sold it to David Holley.*

According to The Bookseller, *edition of 1885, this poem was 'the most popular lyrical poem of the world.']*

Once upon a midnight dreary, while I pondered,
weak and weary,
Over many a quaint and curious volume of forgotten
lore—
While I nodded, nearly napping, suddenly
there came a tapping,
As of some one gently rapping, rapping at my
chamber door.
"'Tis some visitor," I muttered, "tapping at my
chamber door—
Only this and nothing more."

Ah, distinctly I remember it was in the bleak
December;
And each separate dying ember wrought its ghost
upon the floor.
Eagerly I wished the morrow;—vainly I had
sought to borrow

From my books surcease of sorrow—sorrow for
the lost Lenore—
For the rare and radiant maiden whom the angels
name Lenore—
Nameless *here* for evermore.

And the silken, sad, uncertain rustling of each
purple curtain
Thrilled me—filled me with fantastic terrors never felt
before;
So that now, to still the beating of my heart, I
stood repeating
"'Tis some visitor entreating entrance at my
chamber door—
Some late visitor entreating entrance at my chamber
door;—
This it is and nothing more."

Presently my soul grew stronger; hesitating
then no longer,
"Sir," said I, "or Madam, truly your forgiveness I
implore;
But the fact is I was napping, and so gently
you came rapping,

And so faintly you came tapping, tapping at
my chamber door,
That I scarce was sure I heard you"—here I opened
wide the door;—
Darkness there and nothing more.

Deep into that darkness peering, long I stood
there wondering, fearing,
Doubting, dreaming dreams no mortal ever dared to
dream before;
But the silence was unbroken, and the stillness
gave no token,
And the only word there spoken was the
whispered word, "Lenore?"
This I whispered, and an echo murmured back the
word, "Lenore!"—
Merely this and nothing more.

Back into the chamber turning, all my soul
within me burning,
Soon again I heard a tapping somewhat louder than
before.
"Surely," said I, "surely that is something at
my window lattice;

Let me see, then, what thereat is, and this
mystery explore—
Let my heart be still a moment and this mystery
explore;—
'Tis the wind and nothing more!"

Open here I flung the shutter, when, with many
a flirt and flutter,
In there stepped a stately Raven of the saintly days
of yore;
Not the least obeisance made he; not a minute
stopped or stayed he;
But, with mien of lord or lady, perched above
my chamber door—
Perched upon a bust of Pallas[1] just above my
chamber door—
Perched, and sat, and nothing more.

Then this ebony bird beguiling my sad fancy into
smiling,

---

1 Pallas was an epithet given to Athena, the goddess of wisdom. That the raven perches on the bust of Pallas may serve as an indication to the readers than the bird is extraordinary. Though all it is able to say is 'Nevermore', it does come at a time when the man was expecting to see his dead beloved's ghost.

By the grave and stern decorum of the countenance
it wore,
"Though thy crest be shorn and shaven, thou," I said,
"art sure no craven,
Ghastly grim and ancient Raven wandering from the
Nightly shore—
Tell me what thy lordly name is on the Night's
Plutonian shore!"
Quoth the Raven "Nevermore."

Much I marvelled this ungainly fowl to hear
discourse so plainly,
Though its answer little meaning—little relevancy
bore;
For we cannot help agreeing that no living
human being
Ever yet was blessed with seeing bird above
his chamber door—
Bird or beast upon the sculptured bust above his
chamber door,
With such name as "Nevermore."

But the Raven, sitting lonely on the placid
bust, spoke only

That one word, as if his soul in that one word he did
outpour.
Nothing farther then he uttered—not a feather
then he fluttered—
Till I scarcely more than muttered "Other
friends have flown before—
On the morrow *he* will leave me, as my Hopes have
flown before."
Then the bird said "Nevermore."

Startled at the stillness broken by reply so
aptly spoken,
"Doubtless," said I, "what it utters is its only stock
and store
Caught from some unhappy master whom
unmerciful Disaster
Followed fast and followed faster till his songs
one burden bore—
Till the dirges of his Hope that melancholy burden
bore
Of 'Never—nevermore'."

But the Raven still beguiling all my fancy[2] into
smiling,
Straight I wheeled a cushioned seat in front of bird,
and bust and door;
Then, upon the velvet sinking, I betook myself
to linking
Fancy unto fancy, thinking what this ominous
bird of yore—
What this grim, ungainly, ghastly, gaunt, and
ominous bird of yore
Meant in croaking "Nevermore."

This I sat engaged in guessing, but no
syllable expressing
To the fowl whose fiery eyes now burned into my
bosom's core;
This and more I sat divining, with my head at
ease reclining
On the cushion's velvet lining that the lamp-
light gloated o'er,

---

2 An interpretation of the talking bird's existence is that it is only in the mind of the man, and is, therefore, not real. The grief of Lenore's death is eating away at the man to the point of hallucinations. But the fantastical elements are a part and parcel of Gothicism, so a talking bird appearing at the dead of the night might not be a mere illusion.

But whose velvet-violet lining with the lamp-light
gloating o'er,
She shall press, ah, nevermore!

Then, methought, the air grew denser,
perfumed from an unseen censer
Swung by Seraphim whose foot-falls tinkled on the
tufted floor.
"Wretch," I cried, "thy God hath lent thee—by
these angels he hath sent thee
Respite—respite and nepenthe from thy
memories of Lenore;
Quaff, oh quaff this kind nepenthe and forget this
lost Lenore!"
Quoth the Raven "Nevermore."

"Prophet!" said I, "thing of evil!—prophet still,
if bird or devil!—
Whether Tempter sent, or whether tempest tossed
thee here ashore,
Desolate yet all undaunted, on this desert
land enchanted—
On this home by Horror haunted—tell me
truly, I implore—

Is there—*is* there balm in Gilead?—tell me—tell me,
I implore!"
Quoth the Raven "Nevermore."

"Prophet!" said I, "thing of evil!—prophet still,
if bird or devil!
By that Heaven that bends above us—by that God we
both adore—
Tell this soul with sorrow laden if, within the
distant Aidenn,
It shall clasp a sainted maiden whom the
angels name Lenore—
Clasp a rare and radiant maiden whom the angels
name Lenore."
Quoth the Raven "Nevermore."

"Be that word our sign of parting, bird or
fiend!" I shrieked, upstarting—
"Get thee back into the tempest and the Night's
Plutonian shore!
Leave no black plume as a token of that lie thy soul
hath spoken!
Leave my loneliness unbroken!—quit the bust
above my door!

Take thy beak from out my heart, and take thy form
from off my door!"
Quoth the Raven "Nevermore."

And the Raven, never flitting, still is
sitting, *still* is sitting
On the pallid bust of Pallas just above my chamber
door;
And his eyes have all the seeming of a
demon's that is dreaming,
And the lamp-light o'er him streaming throws
his shadow on the floor;
And my soul from out that shadow that lies
floating on the floor
Shall be lifted—nevermore!

The Summer Rain

by Henry David Thoreau

Published 1849

My books I'd fain cast off, I cannot read,
'Twixt every page my thoughts go stray at large
Down in the meadow, where is richer feed,
And will not mind to hit their proper targe.

Plutarch was good, and so was Homer too,
Our Shakespeare's life were rich to live again,
What Plutarch read, that was not good nor true,
Nor Shakespeare's books, unless his books were men.

Here while I lie beneath this walnut bough,
What care I for the Greeks or for Troy town,
If juster battles are enacted now
Between the ants upon this hummock's crown?

Bid Homer wait till I the issue learn,
If red or black the gods will favor most,
Or yonder Ajax will the phalanx turn,
Struggling to heave some rock against the host.

Tell Shakespeare to attend some leisure hour,
For now I've business with this drop of dew,
And see you not, the clouds prepare a shower–
I'll meet him shortly when the sky is blue.

This bed of herd's grass and wild oats was spread
Last year with nicer skill than monarchs use.
A clover tuft is pillow for my head,
And violets quite overtop my shoes.

And now the cordial clouds have shut all in,
And gently swells the wind to say all's well;
The scattered drops are falling fast and thin,
Some in the pool, some in the flower-bell.

I am well drenched upon my bed of oats;
But see that globe come rolling down its stem,
Now like a lonely planet there it floats,
And now it sinks into my garment's hem.

Drip drip the trees for all the country round,
And richness rare distills from every bough;
The wind alone it is makes every sound,
Shaking down crystals on the leaves below.

For shame the sun will never show himself,
Who could not with his beams e'er melt me so;
My dripping locks–they would become an elf,
Who in a beaded coat does gayly go.

How Do I Love Thee

by Elizabeth Barrett Browning

Published in *Sonnets from the Portuguese* (1850)

How do I love thee? Let me count the ways.
I love thee[1] to the depth and breadth and height
My soul can reach, when feeling out of sight
For the ends of being and ideal grace.
I love thee to the level of every day's
Most quiet need, by sun and candle-light.
I love thee freely, as men strive for right.
I love thee purely, as they turn from praise.
I love thee with the passion put to use
In my old griefs, and with my childhood's faith.
I love thee with a love I seemed to lose
With my lost saints. I love thee with the breath,
Smiles, tears, of all my life; and, if God choose,
I shall but love thee better after death.

---

1 This book of love sonnets was dedicated to Elizabeth Barrett's then lover, Robert Browning. The title of the book is misleading, making its readers think that Elizabeth Barrett has only translated these from Portuguese, while in fact, she is the composer. This was deliberately done to mask who these sonnets were intended for. Robert Browning did not know that Elizabeth had written these till 1849. He then urged her to publish them. To this day, the love sonnets remain Elizabeth Barrett Browning's most renowned work.

In Memorian
A. H. H.
(an excerpt)

by Alfred Tennyson

Published 1850

[Arthur Henry Hallam, friend to Alfred Tennyson and an aspiring poet, died of a cerebral haemorrhage in 1833 in Vienna, Italy.

The poem, earlier titled 'The Way of the Soul', was written over a course of seventeen years, and has 133 cantos. The following lines are from Canto 56.]

"So careful of the type?" but no.
From scarped cliff and quarried stone
She cries, "A thousand types are gone:
I care for nothing, all shall go.[1]
"Thou makest thine appeal to me:
I bring to life, I bring to death:
The spirit does but mean the breath:
I know no more." And he, shall he,
Man, her last work, who seem'd so fair,
Such splendid purpose in his eyes,
Who roll'd the psalm to wintry skies,
Who built him fanes of fruitless prayer,
Who trusted God was love indeed
And love Creation's final law—

---

1 The types mean species. So many species had perished, and man will have the same fate. Humans will follow the dinosaurs into extinction.

Tho' Nature, red in tooth and claw[2]
With ravine, shriek'd against his creed—
Who loved, who suffer'd countless ills,
Who battled for the True, the Just,
Be blown about the desert dust,
Or seal'd within the iron hills?
No more? A monster then, a dream,
A discord. Dragons of the prime,
That tare each other in their slime,
Were mellow music match'd with him.

O life as futile, then, as frail!
O for thy voice to soothe and bless!
What hope of answer, or redress?
Behind the veil, behind the veil.

---

2 This line is often quoted in discourses on nature. Here, Tennyson describes the ruthless way nature dispenses of people generation after generation. Though Darwin's *The Origin of Species* came out nine years after this poem was published, this line is often cited as prefiguring his theory of natural selection.

Charge of the Light Brigade

by Alfred Tennyson

Published in

The Examiner (1854)

[The poem is about the charge of the light brigade during the Crimean War (1853-1856). The 1854 Battle of Balaklava inspired Tennyson to write this poem, paying a tribute to the British cavalry that attacked the properly guarded Russian troops, losing many of their soldiers in the process.]

Half a league, half a league,
    Half a league onward,
All in the valley of Death
    Rode the six hundred.
"Forward, the Light Brigade!
Charge for the guns!" he said;
Into the valley of Death
    Rode the six hundred.

"Forward, the Light Brigade!"
Was there a man dismayed?
Not though the soldier knew
    Some one had blundered:
Theirs not to make reply,
Theirs not to reason why,
Theirs but to do and die:
Into the valley of Death
    Rode the six hundred.

Cannon to right of them,
Cannon to left of them,
Cannon in front of them
    Volleyed and thundered;
Stormed at with shot and shell,
Boldly they rode and well;
Into the jaws of Death,
Into the mouth of Hell,
    Rode the six hundred.

Flashed all their sabres bare,
Flashed as they turned in air,
Sabring the gunners there,
Charging an army, while
    All the world wondered:
Plunged in the battery-smoke,
Right through the line they broke:
Cossack and Russian
Reeled from the sabre-stroke,
    Shattered and sundered.
Then they rode back, but not—
    Not the six hundred.

Cannon to right of them,
Cannon to left of them,

Cannon behind them
    Volleyed and thundered:
Stormed at with shot and shell,
While horse and hero fell,
They that had fought so well
Came through the jaws of Death
Back from the mouth of Hell,—
All that was left of them,
    Left of six hundred.

When can their glory fade?
O the wild charge they made!
    All the world wondered.
Honor the charge they made!
Honor the Light Brigade,
    Noble six hundred!

Brahma

by Ralph Waldo Emerson

Published in

Atlantic Monthly (1857)

If the red slayer think he slays,
Or if the slain think he is slain,
They know not well the subtle ways
I keep, and pass, and turn again.

Far or forgot to me is near;
Shadow and sunlight are the same;
The vanished gods to me appear;
And one to me are shame and fame.

They reckon ill who leave me out;
When me they fly, I am the wings;
I am the doubter and the doubt,
I am the hymn the Brahmin sings.

The strong gods pine for my abode,
And pine in vain the sacred Seven;
But thou, meek lover of the good!
Find me, and turn thy back on heaven.

Goblin Market

by Christina Rossetti

Published in *Goblin Market and Other Poems* (1862)

Morning and evening
Maids heard the goblins cry:
"Come buy our orchard fruits,
Come buy, come buy:
Apples and quinces,
Lemons and oranges,
Plump unpeck'd cherries,
Melons and raspberries,
Bloom-down-cheek'd peaches,
Swart-headed mulberries,
Wild free-born cranberries,
Crab-apples, dewberries,
Pine-apples, blackberries,
Apricots, strawberries;—
All ripe together
In summer weather,—
Morns that pass by,
Fair eves that fly;
Come buy, come buy:
Our grapes fresh from the vine,
Pomegranates full and fine,
Dates and sharp bullaces,
Rare pears and greengages,
Damsons and bilberries,
Taste them and try:

Currants and gooseberries,
Bright-fire-like barberries,
Figs to fill your mouth,
Citrons from the South,
Sweet to tongue and sound to eye;
Come buy, come buy."

Evening by evening
Among the brookside rushes,
Laura bow'd her head to hear,
Lizzie veil'd her blushes:
Crouching close together
In the cooling weather,
With clasping arms and cautioning lips,
With tingling cheeks and finger tips.
"Lie close," Laura said,
Pricking up her golden head:
"We must not look at goblin men,
We must not buy their fruits:
Who knows upon what soil they fed
Their hungry thirsty roots?"
"Come buy," call the goblins
Hobbling down the glen.

"Oh," cried Lizzie, "Laura, Laura,
You should not peep[1] at goblin men."
Lizzie cover'd up her eyes,
Cover'd close lest they should look;
Laura rear'd her glossy head,
And whisper'd like the restless brook:
"Look, Lizzie, look, Lizzie,
Down the glen tramp little men.
One hauls a basket,
One bears a plate,
One lugs a golden dish
Of many pounds weight.
How fair the vine must grow
Whose grapes are so luscious;
How warm the wind must blow
Through those fruit bushes."
"No," said Lizzie, "No, no, no;
Their offers should not charm us,
Their evil gifts would harm us."
She thrust a dimpled finger
In each ear, shut eyes and ran:

1 The poem's earlier title was 'Peeping at the Goblins'.

Curious Laura chose to linger[2]
Wondering at each merchant man.
One had a cat's face,
One whisk'd a tail,
One tramp'd at a rat's pace,
One crawl'd like a snail,
One like a wombat prowl'd obtuse and furry,
One like a ratel tumbled hurry skurry.
She heard a voice like voice of doves
Cooing all together:
They sounded kind and full of loves
In the pleasant weather.
Laura stretch'd her gleaming neck
Like a rush-imbedded swan,
Like a lily from the beck,
Like a moonlit poplar branch,
Like a vessel at the launch
When its last restraint is gone.

Backwards up the mossy glen
Turn'd and troop'd the goblin men,
With their shrill repeated cry,

---

2 The two sisters are poles apart in this. Lizzie is cautious, but Laura is daring.

"Come buy, come buy."
When they reach'd where Laura was
They stood stock still upon the moss,
Leering at each other,
Brother with queer brother;
Signalling each other,
Brother with sly brother.
One set his basket down,
One rear'd his plate;
One began to weave a crown
Of tendrils, leaves, and rough nuts brown
(Men sell not such in any town);
One heav'd the golden weight
Of dish and fruit to offer her:
"Come buy, come buy," was still their cry.
Laura stared but did not stir,
Long'd but had no money:
The whisk-tail'd merchant bade her taste
In tones as smooth as honey,
The cat-faced purr'd,
The rat-faced spoke a word
Of welcome, and the snail-paced even was heard;
One parrot-voiced and jolly
Cried "Pretty Goblin" still for "Pretty Polly;"—
One whistled like a bird.

But sweet-tooth Laura spoke in haste:
"Good folk, I have no coin;
To take were to purloin:
I have no copper in my purse,
I have no silver either,
And all my gold is on the furze
That shakes in windy weather
Above the rusty heather."
"You have much gold upon your head,"
They answer'd all together:
"Buy from us with a golden curl."
She clipp'd a precious golden lock,
She dropp'd a tear more rare than pearl,
Then suck'd their fruit globes fair or red:
Sweeter than honey from the rock,
Stronger than man-rejoicing wine,
Clearer than water flow'd that juice;
She never tasted such before,
How should it cloy with length of use?
She suck'd and suck'd and suck'd the more
Fruits which that unknown orchard bore;
She suck'd until her lips were sore;
Then flung the emptied rinds away
But gather'd up one kernel stone,

And knew not was it night or day
As she turn'd home alone.

Lizzie met her at the gate
Full of wise upbraidings:
"Dear, you should not stay so late,
Twilight is not good for maidens;
Should not loiter in the glen
In the haunts of goblin men.
Do you not remember Jeanie,[3]
How she met them in the moonlight,
Took their gifts both choice and many,
Ate their fruits and wore their flowers
Pluck'd from bowers
Where summer ripens at all hours?
But ever in the noonlight
She pined and pined away;
Sought them by night and day,
Found them no more, but dwindled and grew grey;
Then fell with the first snow,
While to this day no grass will grow

---

3 This is often cited as a reference to Dante Gabriel Rossetti's poem 'Jenny', in which Jenny is a prostitute. So the reference would imply that her prostitution was a result of her encounter with the goblins.

Where she lies low:
I planted daisies there a year ago
That never blow.
You should not loiter so."
"Nay, hush," said Laura:
"Nay, hush, my sister:
I ate and ate my fill,
Yet my mouth waters still;
To-morrow night I will
Buy more;" and kiss'd her:
"Have done with sorrow;
I'll bring you plums to-morrow
Fresh on their mother twigs,
Cherries worth getting;
You cannot think what figs
My teeth have met in,
What melons icy-cold
Piled on a dish of gold
Too huge for me to hold,
What peaches with a velvet nap,
Pellucid grapes without one seed:
Odorous indeed must be the mead
Whereon they grow, and pure the wave they drink
With lilies at the brink,
And sugar-sweet their sap."

Golden head by golden head,
Like two pigeons in one nest
Folded in each other's wings,
They lay down in their curtain'd bed:
Like two blossoms on one stem,
Like two flakes of new-fall'n snow,
Like two wands of ivory
Tipp'd with gold for awful kings.
Moon and stars gaz'd in at them,
Wind sang to them lullaby,
Lumbering owls forbore to fly,
Not a bat flapp'd to and fro
Round their rest:
Cheek to cheek and breast to breast
Lock'd together in one nest.

Early in the morning
When the first cock crow'd his warning,
Neat like bees, as sweet and busy,
Laura rose with Lizzie:
Fetch'd in honey, milk'd the cows,
Air'd and set to rights the house,
Kneaded cakes of whitest wheat,
Cakes for dainty mouths to eat,
Next churn'd butter, whipp'd up cream,

Fed their poultry, sat and sew'd;
Talk'd as modest maidens should:
Lizzie with an open heart,
Laura in an absent dream,
One content, one sick in part;
One warbling for the mere bright day's delight,
One longing for the night.

At length slow evening came:
They went with pitchers to the reedy brook;
Lizzie most placid in her look,
Laura most like a leaping flame.
They drew the gurgling water from its deep;
Lizzie pluck'd purple and rich golden flags,
Then turning homeward said: "The sunset
    flushes
Those furthest loftiest crags;
Come, Laura, not another maiden lags.
No wilful squirrel wags,
The beasts and birds are fast asleep."
But Laura loiter'd still among the rushes
And said the bank was steep.

And said the hour was early still
The dew not fall'n, the wind not chill;

Listening ever, but not catching
The customary cry,
"Come buy, come buy,"
With its iterated jingle
Of sugar-baited words:
Not for all her watching
Once discerning even one goblin
Racing, whisking, tumbling, hobbling;
Let alone the herds
That used to tramp along the glen,
In groups or single,
Of brisk fruit-merchant men.

Till Lizzie urged, "O Laura, come;
I hear the fruit-call but I dare not look:
You should not loiter longer at this brook:
Come with me home.
The stars rise, the moon bends her arc,
Each glowworm winks her spark,
Let us get home before the night grows dark:
For clouds may gather
Though this is summer weather,
Put out the lights and drench us through;
Then if we lost our way what should we do?"

Laura turn'd cold as stone
To find her sister heard that cry alone,
That goblin cry,
"Come buy our fruits,[4] come buy."
Must she then buy no more such dainty fruit?
Must she no more such succous pasture find,
Gone deaf and blind?
Her tree of life droop'd from the root:
She said not one word in her heart's sore ache;
But peering thro' the dimness, nought discerning,
Trudg'd home, her pitcher dripping all the way;
So crept to bed, and lay
Silent till Lizzie slept;
Then sat up in a passionate yearning,
And gnash'd her teeth for baulk'd desire, and wept
As if her heart would break.

Day after day, night after night,
Laura kept watch in vain
In sullen silence of exceeding pain.
She never caught again the goblin cry:

4 Using of the fruits by goblins to lure women, has often been cited to be similar to Satan tempting Eve to eat the forbidden fruit. Just like Eve eats the fruit and is then ruined, so is Laura.

"Come buy, come buy;"—
She never spied the goblin men
Hawking their fruits along the glen:
But when the noon wax'd bright
Her hair grew thin and grey;
She dwindled, as the fair full moon doth turn
To swift decay and burn
Her fire away.

One day remembering her kernel-stone
She set it by a wall that faced the south;
Dew'd it with tears, hoped for a root,
Watch'd for a waxing shoot,
But there came none;
It never saw the sun,
It never felt the trickling moisture run:
While with sunk eyes and faded mouth
She dream'd of melons, as a traveller sees
False waves in desert drouth
With shade of leaf-crown'd trees,
And burns the thirstier in the sandful breeze.

She no more swept the house,
Tended the fowls or cows,
Fetch'd honey, kneaded cakes of wheat,

Brought water from the brook:
But sat down listless in the chimney-nook
And would not eat.

Tender Lizzie could not bear
To watch her sister's cankerous care
Yet not to share.
She night and morning
Caught the goblins' cry:
"Come buy our orchard fruits,
Come buy, come buy;"—
Beside the brook, along the glen,
She heard the tramp of goblin men,
The yoke and stir
Poor Laura could not hear;
Long'd to buy fruit to comfort her,
But fear'd to pay too dear.
She thought of Jeanie in her grave,
Who should have been a bride;
But who for joys brides hope to have
Fell sick and died
In her gay prime,
In earliest winter time
With the first glazing rime,
With the first snow-fall of crisp winter time.

Till Laura dwindling
Seem'd knocking at Death's door:
Then Lizzie weigh'd no more
Better and worse;
But put a silver penny in her purse,
Kiss'd Laura, cross'd the heath with clumps of furze
At twilight, halted by the brook:
And for the first time in her life
Began to listen and look.

Laugh'd every goblin
When they spied her peeping:
Came towards her hobbling,
Flying, running, leaping,
Puffing and blowing,
Chuckling, clapping, crowing,
Clucking and gobbling,
Mopping and mowing,
Full of airs and graces,
Pulling wry faces,
Demure grimaces,
Cat-like and rat-like,
Ratel- and wombat-like,
Snail-paced in a hurry,
Parrot-voiced and whistler,

Helter skelter, hurry skurry,
Chattering like magpies,
Fluttering like pigeons,
Gliding like fishes,—
Hugg'd her and kiss'd her:
Squeez'd and caress'd her:
Stretch'd up their dishes,
Panniers, and plates:
"Look at our apples
Russet and dun,
Bob at our cherries,
Bite at our peaches,
Citrons and dates,
Grapes for the asking,
Pears red with basking
Out in the sun,
Plums on their twigs;
Pluck them and suck them,
Pomegranates, figs."—

"Good folk," said Lizzie,
Mindful of Jeanie:
"Give me much and many: —
Held out her apron,
Toss'd them her penny.

"Nay, take a seat with us,
Honour and eat with us,"
They answer'd grinning:
"Our feast is but beginning.
Night yet is early,
Warm and dew-pearly,
Wakeful and starry:
Such fruits as these
No man can carry:
Half their bloom would fly,
Half their dew would dry,
Halt their flavour would pass by.
Sit down and feast with us,
Be welcome guest with us,
Cheer you and rest with us."—
"Thank you," said Lizzie: "But one waits
At home alone for me:
So without further parleying,
If you will not sell me any
Of your fruits though much and many,
Give me back my silver penny
I toss'd you for a fee."—
They began to scratch their pates,
No longer wagging, purring,
But visibly demurring,

Grunting and snarling.
One call'd her proud,
Cross-grain'd, uncivil;
Their tones wax'd loud,
Their looks were evil.
Lashing their tails
They trod and hustled her,
Elbow'd and jostled her,
Claw'd with their nails,
Barking, mewing, hissing, mocking,
Tore her gown and soil'd her stocking,
Twitch'd her hair out by the roots,
Stamp'd upon her tender feet,
Held her hands and squeez'd their fruits
Against her mouth to make her eat.

White and golden Lizzie stood,
Like a lily in a flood,—
Like a rock of blue-vein'd stone
Lash'd by tides obstreperously,—
Like a beacon left alone
In a hoary roaring sea,
Sending up a golden fire,—
Like a fruit-crown'd orange-tree
White with blossoms honey-sweet

Sore beset by wasp and bee,—
Like a royal virgin town
Topp'd with gilded dome and spire
Close beleaguer'd by a fleet
Mad to tug her standard down.

One may lead a horse to water,
Twenty cannot make him drink.
Though the goblins cuff'd and caught her,
Coax'd and fought her,
Bullied and besought her,
Scratch'd her, pinch'd her black as ink,
Kick'd and knock'd her,
Maul'd and mock'd her,
Lizzie utter'd not a word;[5]
Would not open lip from lip
Lest they should cram a mouthful in:
But laugh'd in heart to feel the drip
Of juice that syrupp'd all her face,
And lodg'd in dimples of her chin,
And streak'd her neck which quaked like curd.
At last the evil people,

---

5 Lizzie could safeguard her chastity since saving her sister, and not her desire, brought her to the market.

Worn out by her resistance,
Flung back her penny, kick'd their fruit
Along whichever road they took,
Not leaving root or stone or shoot;
Some writh'd into the ground,
Some div'd into the brook
With ring and ripple,
Some scudded on the gale without a sound,
Some vanish'd in the distance.

In a smart, ache, tingle,
Lizzie went her way;
Knew not was it night or day;
Sprang up the bank, tore thro' the furze,
Threaded copse and dingle,
And heard her penny jingle
Bouncing in her purse,—
Its bounce was music to her ear.
She ran and ran
As if she fear'd some goblin man
Dogg'd her with gibe or curse
Or something worse:
But not one goblin scurried after,
Nor was she prick'd by fear;
The kind heart made her windy-paced

That urged her home quite out of breath with haste
And inward laughter.

She cried, "Laura," up the garden,
"Did you miss me?
Come and kiss me.
Never mind my bruises,
Hug me, kiss me, suck my juices
Squeez'd from goblin fruits for you,
Goblin pulp and goblin dew.
Eat me, drink me, love me;
Laura, make much of me;
For your sake I have braved the glen
And had to do with goblin merchant men."

Laura started from her chair,
Flung her arms up in the air,
Clutch'd her hair:
"Lizzie, Lizzie, have you tasted
For my sake the fruit forbidden?
Must your light like mine be hidden,
Your young life like mine be wasted,
Undone in mine undoing,
And ruin'd in my ruin,
Thirsty, canker'd, goblin-ridden?"—

She clung about her sister,
Kiss'd and kiss'd and kiss'd her:
Tears once again
Refresh'd her shrunken eyes,
Dropping like rain
After long sultry drouth;
Shaking with aguish fear, and pain,
She kiss'd and kiss'd her with a hungry mouth.
Her lips began to scorch,

That juice was wormwood to her tongue,
She loath'd the feast:
Writhing as one possess'd she leap'd and sung,
Rent all her robe, and wrung
Her hands in lamentable haste,
And beat her breast.
Her locks stream'd like the torch
Borne by a racer at full speed,
Or like the mane of horses in their flight,
Or like an eagle when she stems the light
Straight toward the sun,
Or like a caged thing freed,
Or like a flying flag when armies run.

Swift fire spread through her veins, knock'd at
her heart,
Met the fire smouldering there
And overbore its lesser flame;
She gorged on bitterness without a name:
Ah! fool, to choose such part
Of soul-consuming care!
Sense fail'd in the mortal strife:
Like the watch-tower of a town
Which an earthquake shatters down,
Like a lightning-stricken mast,
Like a wind-uprooted tree
Spun about,
Like a foam-topp'd waterspout
Cast down headlong in the sea,
She fell at last;
Pleasure past and anguish past,
Is it death or is it life?

Life out of death.
That night long Lizzie watch'd by her,
Counted her pulse's flagging stir,
Felt for her breath,
Held water to her lips, and cool'd her face
With tears and fanning leaves:

But when the first birds chirp'd about their eaves,
And early reapers plodded to the place
Of golden sheaves,
And dew-wet grass
Bow'd in the morning winds so brisk to pass,
And new buds with new day
Open'd of cup-like lilies on the stream,
Laura awoke as from a dream,
Laugh'd in the innocent old way,
Hugg'd Lizzie but not twice or thrice;
Her gleaming locks show'd not one thread of grey,
Her breath was sweet as May
And light danced in her eyes.

Days, weeks, months, years
Afterwards, when both were wives
With children of their own;
Their mother-hearts beset with fears,
Their lives bound up in tender lives;
Laura would call the little ones
And tell them of her early prime,
Those pleasant days long gone
Of not-returning time:
Would talk about the haunted glen,
The wicked, quaint fruit-merchant men,

Their fruits like honey to the throat
But poison in the blood;
(Men sell not such in any town):
Would tell them how her sister stood
In deadly peril to do her good,
And win the fiery antidote:
Then joining hands to little hands
Would bid them cling together,
"For there is no friend like a sister
In calm or stormy weather;
To cheer one on the tedious way,
To fetch one if one goes astray,
To lift one if one totters down,
To strengthen whilst one stands."

Rabbi Ben Ezra

by Robert Browning

Published in

Dramatis Personae (1864)

Grow old along with me![1]
The best is yet to be,
The last of life, for which the first was made:
Our times are in His hand
Who saith "A whole I planned,
Youth shows but half; trust God: see all, nor be afraid!"

Not that, amassing flowers,
Youth sighed "Which rose make ours,
Which lily leave and then as best recall?"
Not that, admiring stars,
It yearned "Nor Jove, nor Mars;
Mine be some figured flame which blends,
transcends them all!"

Not for such hopes and fears
Annulling youth's brief years,
Do I remonstrate: folly wide the mark!
Rather I prize the doubt
Low kinds exist without,
Finished and finite clods, untroubled by a spark.

---

1 Another one of Browning's dramatic monologues, where the speaker is Rabbi Abraham ben Meir ibn Ezra. Though unlike other speakers in Browning's monologues, this speaker was real He was a twelfth century scholar, poet, and mathematician.

Poor vaunt of life indeed,
Were man but formed to feed
On joy, to solely seek and find and feast:
Such feasting ended, then
As sure an end to men;
Irks care the crop-full bird? Frets doubt the maw-
crammed beast?

Rejoice we are allied
To That which doth provide
And not partake, effect and not receive!
A spark disturbs our clod;
Nearer we hold of God
Who gives, than of His tribes that take, I must believe.

Then, welcome each rebuff
That turns earth's smoothness rough,
Each sting that bids nor sit nor stand but go!
Be our joys three-parts pain!
Strive, and hold cheap the strain;
Learn, nor account the pang; dare, never grudge
the throe!

For thence,—a paradox
Which comforts while it mocks,—

Shall life succeed in that it seems to fail:
What I aspired to be,
And was not, comforts me:
A brute I might have been, but would not sink i' the scale.

What is he but a brute
Whose flesh has soul to suit,
Whose spirit works lest arms and legs want play?
To man, propose this test—
Thy body at its best,
How far can that project thy soul on its lone way?

Yet gifts should prove their use:
I own the Past profuse
Of power each side, perfection every turn:
Eyes, ears took in their dole,
Brain treasured up the whole;
Should not the heart beat once "How good to live and learn?"

Not once beat "Praise be Thine!
I see the whole design,
I, who saw power, see now love perfect too:
Perfect I call Thy plan:

Thanks that I was a man!
Maker, remake, complete,—I trust what
Thou shalt do!"

For pleasant is this flesh;
Our soul, in its rose-mesh
Pulled ever to the earth, still yearns for rest;
Would we some prize might hold
To match those manifold
Possessions of the brute,—gain most, as we did best!

Let us not always say,
"Spite of this flesh to-day
I strove, made head, gained ground upon the whole!"
As the bird wings and sings,
Let us cry "All good things
Are ours, nor soul helps flesh more, now, than
flesh helps soul!"

Therefore I summon age
To grant youth's heritage,
Life's struggle having so far reached its term:
Thence shall I pass, approved
A man, for aye removed
From the developed brute; a god though in the germ.

And I shall thereupon
Take rest, ere I be gone
Once more on my adventure brave and new:
Fearless and unperplexed,
When I wage battle next,
What weapons to select, what armour to indue.

Youth ended, I shall try
My gain or loss thereby;
Leave the fire ashes, what survives is gold:
And I shall weigh the same,
Give life its praise or blame:
Young, all lay in dispute; I shall know, being old.

For note, when evening shuts,
A certain moment cuts
The deed off, calls the glory from the grey:
A whisper from the west
Shoots—"Add this to the rest,
Take it and try its worth: here dies another day."

So, still within this life,
Though lifted o'er its strife,
Let me discern, compare, pronounce at last,
This rage was right i' the main,

That acquiescence vain:
The Future I may face now I have proved the Past."

For more is not reserved
To man, with soul just nerved
To act to-morrow what he learns to-day:
Here, work enough to watch
The Master work, and catch
Hints of the proper craft, tricks of the tool's true play.

As it was better, youth
Should strive, through acts uncouth,
Toward making, than repose on aught found made:
So, better, age, exempt
From strife, should know, than tempt
Further. Thou waitedst age: wait death nor be afraid!

Enough now, if the Right
And Good and Infinite
Be named here, as thou callest thy hand thine own
With knowledge absolute,
Subject to no dispute
From fools that crowded youth, nor let thee
feel alone.

Be there, for once and all,
Severed great minds from small,
Announced to each his station in the Past!
Was I, the world arraigned,
Were they, my soul disdained,
Right? Let age speak the truth and give us peace
at last!

Now, who shall arbitrate?
Ten men love what I hate,
Shun what I follow, slight what I receive;
Ten, who in ears and eyes
Match me: we all surmise,
They this thing, and I that: whom shall my soul
believe?

Not on the vulgar mass
Called "work," must sentence pass,
Things done, that took the eye and had the price;
O'er which, from level stand,
The low world laid its hand,
Found straightway to its mind, could value in a trice:

But all, the world's coarse thumb
And finger failed to plumb,

So passed in making up the main account;
All instincts immature,
All purposes unsure,
That weighed not as his work, yet swelled the
 man's amount:

Thoughts hardly to be packed
Into a narrow act,
Fancies that broke through language and escaped;
All I could never be,
All, men ignored in me,
This, I was worth to God, whose wheel the pitcher
 shaped.

Ay, note that Potter's wheel,[2]
That metaphor! and feel
Why time spins fast, why passive lies our clay,—
Thou, to whom fools propound,
When the wine makes its round,
"Since life fleets, all is change; the Past gone,
 seize to-day!"

---

2 This metaphor had also been used in *The Rubaiyyat of Omar Khayyam*. In direct contrast to the hedonism in that book, this poem's speaker rejects succumbing to small pleasures and instead gives importance to life's trials that lead to spiritual development.

Fool! All that is, at all,
Lasts ever, past recall;
Earth changes, but thy soul and God stand sure:
What entered into thee,
That was, is, and shall be:
Time's wheel runs back or stops: Potter and
clay endure.

He fixed thee mid this dance
Of plastic circumstance,
This Present, thou, forsooth, wouldst fain arrest:
Machinery just meant
To give thy soul its bent,
Try thee and turn thee forth, sufficiently impressed.

What though the earlier grooves,
Which ran the laughing loves
Around thy base, no longer pause and press?
What though, about thy rim,
Skull-things in order grim
Grow out, in graver mood, obey the sterner stress?

Look not thou down but up!
To uses of a cup,
The festal board, lamp's flash and trumpet's peal,

The new wine's foaming flow,
The Master's lips a-glow!
Thou, heaven's consummate cup, what need'st thou
with earth's wheel?

But I need, now as then,
Thee, God, who mouldest men;
And since, not even while the whirl was worst,
Did I,—to the wheel of life
With shapes and colours rife,
Bound dizzily,—mistake my end, to slake Thy thirst:

So, take and use Thy work:
Amend what flaws may lurk,
What strain o' the stuff, what warpings past the aim!
My times be in Thy hand!
Perfect the cup as planned!
Let age approve of youth, and death complete
the same!

Jabberwocky

by Lewis Carroll

Published in *Through the Looking Glass* (1865)

[Alice travelled into an inverted dream world in which she encountered a book written in an unknown language. The book could only be read when held up against the mirror.

The poem is about killing Jabberwock. Interpretations of the poems are wide-ranging, but it is popularly termed as a nonsense poem.]

'Twas brillig, and the slithy toves
    Did gyre and gimble in the wabe:
All mimsy were the borogoves,
    And the mome raths outgrabe.

"Beware the Jabberwock, my son!
    The jaws that bite, the claws that catch!
Beware the Jubjub bird, and shun
    The frumious Bandersnatch!"

He took his vorpal sword in hand;
    Long time the manxome foe he sought—
So rested he by the Tumtum tree
    And stood awhile in thought.

And, as in uffish thought he stood,
    The Jabberwock, with eyes of flame,

Came whiffling through the tulgey wood,
    And burbled as it came!

One, two! One, two! And through and through
    The vorpal blade went snicker-snack!
He left it dead, and with its head
    He went galumphing back.

"And hast thou slain the Jabberwock?
    Come to my arms, my beamish boy!
O frabjous day! Callooh! Callay!"
    He chortled in his joy.

'Twas brillig, and the slithy toves
    Did gyre and gimble in the wabe:
All mimsy were the borogoves,
    And the mome raths outgrabe.

Dover Beach

by Matthew Arnold

Published in *New Poems* (1867)

The sea is calm tonight.
The tide is full, the moon lies fair
Upon the straits; on the French coast the light
Gleams and is gone; the cliffs of England stand,
Glimmering and vast, out in the tranquil bay.
Come to the window, sweet is the night-air!
Only, from the long line of spray
Where the sea meets the moon-blanched land,
Listen! you hear the grating roar
Of pebbles which the waves draw back, and fling,
At their return, up the high strand,
Begin, and cease, and then again begin,
With tremulous cadence slow, and bring
The eternal note of sadness in.

Sophocles long ago
Heard it on the Ægean,[1] and it brought
Into his mind the turbid ebb and flow
Of human misery;[2] we

---

1 The poet here says that Sophocles heard the same sound that the poet did, and that inspired him to write his legendary tragic plays. Sophocles was a Greek writer who began writing around 468 BCE. His plays are widely read and studied even today.

2 Melancholic tone of the poem is apparent. Here, Arnold projects sadness and misery onto the sea. This projecting of human emotions on inanimate objects is termed as a pathetic fallacy.

Find also in the sound a thought,
Hearing it by this distant northern sea.

The Sea of Faith
Was once, too, at the full, and round earth's shore
Lay like the folds of a bright girdle furled.
But now I only hear
Its melancholy, long, withdrawing roar,
Retreating, to the breath
Of the night-wind, down the vast edges drear
And naked shingles of the world.

Ah, love, let us be true
To one another! for the world, which seems
To lie before us like a land of dreams,
So various, so beautiful, so new,
Hath really neither joy, nor love, nor light,
Nor certitude, nor peace, nor help for pain;
And we are here as on a darkling plain
Swept with confused alarms of struggle and flight,
Where ignorant armies clash by night.

O Captain! My Captain!

by Walt Whitman
Published in
Leaves of Grass (1867)

O Captain! my Captain! our fearful trip is done,
The ship has weather'd every rack, the prize we
sought is won,[1]
The port is near, the bells I hear, the people all
exulting,
While follow eyes the steady keel, the vessel grim
and daring;
But O heart! heart! heart!
O the bleeding drops of red,[2]
Where on the deck my Captain lies,
Fallen cold and dead.

O Captain! my Captain! rise up and hear the bells;
Rise up—for you the flag is flung—for you the
bugle trills,
For you bouquets and ribbon'd wreaths—for you the
shores a-crowding,
For you they call, the swaying mass, their eager
faces turning;

---

1 The prize won might be a reference to the abolishment of slavery. Lincoln had passed the Emancipation Proclamation in 1863. The slaveholders in the southern states were unhappy, people in the northern states were skeptical, and the slaves were jubilant.

2 The poem is about Abraham Lincoln's death. Two years before this poem was published, John Wilkes, a Confederate sympathizer, assassinated Lincoln, shooting him in the head.

Here Captain! dear father!
This arm beneath your head!
It is some dream that on the deck,
You've fallen cold and dead.

My Captain does not answer, his lips are pale
and still,
My father does not feel my arm, he has no pulse
nor will,
The ship is anchor'd safe and sound, its voyage
closed and done,
From fearful trip the victor ship comes in with
object won;
Exult O shores, and ring O bells!
But I with mournful tread,
Walk the deck my Captain lies,
Fallen cold and dead.

This Is My Letter to the World

by Emily Dickinson

Published 1890

This is my letter to the world,[1]
    That never wrote to me,—
The simple news that Nature told,
    With tender majesty.

Her message is committed
    To hands I cannot see;
For love of her, sweet countrymen,
    Judge tenderly of me!

---

1 This poem comes under the category of meta-poetry—a poem about poetry.

The Ballad of Reading Gaol

by Oscar Wilde

Published 1898

[Oscar Wilde was in jail from 1895 to 1897. His crime was being in relationships with men. Accused of gross indecency, Wilde was convicted in the trial since there was enough evidence to prove that he was guilty. Affected by his time in prison, Wilde chose to spent the rest of his remaining life in exile.

This poem was composed when Oscar Wilde was imprisoned at Reading Gaol.]

I.

He did not wear his scarlet coat,
    For blood and wine are red,
And blood and wine were on his hands
    When they found him with the dead,
The poor dead woman whom he loved,
    And murdered in her bed.

He walked amongst the Trial Men
    In a suit of shabby grey;
A cricket cap was on his head,
    And his step seemed light and gay;
But I never saw a man who looked
    So wistfully at the day.

I never saw a man who looked
    With such a wistful eye
Upon that little tent of blue
    Which prisoners call the sky,
And at every drifting cloud that went
    With sails of silver by.

I walked, with other souls in pain,
    Within another ring,
And was wondering if the man had done
    A great or little thing,
When a voice behind me whispered low,
    "That fellow's got to swing."

Dear Christ! the very prison walls
    Suddenly seemed to reel,
And the sky above my head became
    Like a casque of scorching steel;
And, though I was a soul in pain,
    My pain I could not feel.

I only knew what hunted thought
    Quickened his step, and why
He looked upon the garish day
    With such a wistful eye;

The man had killed the thing he loved
    And so he had to die.

Yet each man kills the thing he loves[1]
    By each let this be heard,
Some do it with a bitter look,
    Some with a flattering word,
The coward does it with a kiss,
    The brave man with a sword!

Some kill their love when they are young,
    And some when they are old;
Some strangle with the hands of Lust,
    Some with the hands of Gold:
The kindest use a knife, because
    The dead so soon grow cold.

Some love too little, some too long,
    Some sell, and others buy;
Some do the deed with many tears,

---

1 During Oscar Wilde's trial, he was accused of being in 'love that dare not speak its name.' This line is from a poem *Two Loves* by Alfred Douglas. Douglas, an aspiring British poet, was Wilde's lover.

And some without a sigh:
For each man kills the thing he loves,
Yet each man does not die.

He does not die a death of shame
On a day of dark disgrace,
Nor have a noose about his neck,
Nor a cloth upon his face,
Nor drop feet foremost through the floor
Into an empty place

He does not sit with silent[2] men
Who watch him night and day;
Who watch him when he tries to weep,
And when he tries to pray;
Who watch him lest himself should rob
The prison of its prey.

He does not wake at dawn to see
Dread figures throng his room,
The shivering Chaplain robed in white,
The Sheriff stern with gloom,

---

2 In the nineteenth century, prisoners were not even allowed to talk to each other.

And the Governor all in shiny black,
With the yellow face of Doom.

He does not rise in piteous haste
To put on convict-clothes,
While some coarse-mouthed Doctor gloats, and notes
Each new and nerve-twitched pose,
Fingering a watch whose little ticks
Are like horrible hammer-blows.

He does not know that sickening thirst
That sands one's throat, before
The hangman with his gardener's gloves
Slips through the padded door,
And binds one with three leathern thongs,
That the throat may thirst no more.

He does not bend his head to hear
The Burial Office read,
Nor, while the terror of his soul
Tells him he is not dead,
Cross his own coffin, as he moves
Into the hideous shed.

He does not stare upon the air
    Through a little roof of glass;
He does not pray with lips of clay
    For his agony to pass;
Nor feel upon his shuddering cheek
    The kiss of Caiaphas.

II.

Six weeks our guardsman walked the yard,
    In a suit of shabby grey:
His cricket cap was on his head,
    And his step seemed light and gay,
But I never saw a man who looked
    So wistfully at the day.

I never saw a man who looked
    With such a wistful eye
Upon that little tent of blue
    Which prisoners call the sky,
And at every wandering cloud that trailed
    Its raveled fleeces by.

He did not wring his hands, as do
    Those witless men who dare

To try to rear the changeling Hope
    In the cave of black Despair:
He only looked upon the sun,
    And drank the morning air.

He did not wring his hands nor weep,
    Nor did he peek or pine,
But he drank the air as though it held
    Some healthful anodyne;
With open mouth he drank the sun
    As though it had been wine!

And I and all the souls in pain,
    Who tramped the other ring,
Forgot if we ourselves had done
    A great or little thing,
And watched with gaze of dull amaze
    The man who had to swing.

And strange it was to see him pass
    With a step so light and gay,
And strange it was to see him look
    So wistfully at the day,
And strange it was to think that he
    Had such a debt to pay.

For oak and elm have pleasant leaves
    That in the spring-time shoot:
But grim to see is the gallows-tree,
    With its adder-bitten root,
And, green or dry, a man must die
    Before it bears its fruit!

The loftiest place is that seat of grace
    For which all worldlings try:
But who would stand in hempen band
    Upon a scaffold high,
And through a murderer's collar take
    His last look at the sky?

It is sweet to dance to violins
    When Love and Life are fair:
To dance to flutes, to dance to lutes
    Is delicate and rare:
But it is not sweet with nimble feet
    To dance upon the air!

So with curious eyes and sick surmise
    We watched him day by day,
And wondered if each one of us

Would end the self-same way,
For none can tell to what red Hell
His sightless soul may stray.

At last the dead man walked no more
Amongst the Trial Men,
And I knew that he was standing up
In the black dock's dreadful pen,
And that never would I see his face
In God's sweet world again.

Like two doomed ships that pass in storm
We had crossed each other's way:
But we made no sign, we said no word,
We had no word to say;
For we did not meet in the holy night,
But in the shameful day.

A prison wall was round us both,
Two outcast men were we:
The world had thrust us from its heart,
And God from out His care:
And the iron gin that waits for Sin
Had caught us in its snare.

III.

In Debtors' Yard the stones are hard,
And the dripping wall is high,
So it was there he took the air
Beneath the leaden sky,
And by each side a Warder walked,
For fear the man might die.

Or else he sat with those who watched
His anguish night and day;
Who watched him when he rose to weep,
And when he crouched to pray;
Who watched him lest himself should rob
Their scaffold of its prey.

The Governor was strong upon
The Regulations Act:
The Doctor said that Death was but
A scientific fact:
And twice a day the Chaplain called
And left a little tract.

And twice a day he smoked his pipe,
And drank his quart of beer:

His soul was resolute, and held
No hiding-place for fear;
He often said that he was glad
The hangman's hands were near.

But why he said so strange a thing
No Warder dared to ask:
For he to whom a watcher's doom
Is given as his task,
Must set a lock upon his lips,
And make his face a mask.

Or else he might be moved, and try
To comfort or console:
And what should Human Pity do
Pent up in Murderers' Hole?
What word of grace in such a place
Could help a brother's soul?

With slouch and swing around the ring
We trod the Fool's Parade!
We did not care: we knew we were
The Devil's Own Brigade:
And shaven head and feet of lead
Make a merry masquerade.

We tore the tarry rope[3] to shreds
With blunt and bleeding nails;
We rubbed the doors, and scrubbed the floors,
And cleaned the shining rails:
And, rank by rank, we soaped the plank,
And clattered with the pails.

We sewed the sacks, we broke the stones,
We turned the dusty drill:
We banged the tins, and bawled the hymns,
And sweated on the mill:
But in the heart of every man
Terror was lying still.

So still it lay that every day
Crawled like a weed-clogged wave:
And we forgot the bitter lot
That waits for fool and knave,
Till once, as we tramped in from work,
We passed an open grave.

---

3 Though Wilde had been sentenced to do physical labour in the jail, he was too weak to do any hard, back-breaking work. He was first assigned to pick up oakum, in which he only had to unravel ropes into strands. Later, he was to distribute books from the prison library.

With yawning mouth the yellow hole
    Gaped for a living thing;
The very mud cried out for blood
    To the thirsty asphalte ring:
And we knew that ere one dawn grew fair
    Some prisoner had to swing.

Right in we went, with soul intent
    On Death and Dread and Doom:
The hangman, with his little bag,
    Went shuffling through the gloom
And each man trembled as he crept
    Into his numbered tomb.

That night the empty corridors
    Were full of forms of Fear,
And up and down the iron town
    Stole feet we could not hear,
And through the bars that hide the stars
    White faces seemed to peer.

He lay as one who lies and dreams
    In a pleasant meadow-land,
The watcher watched him as he slept,
    And could not understand

How one could sleep so sweet a sleep
With a hangman close at hand?

But there is no sleep when men must weep
Who never yet have wept:
So we—the fool, the fraud, the knave—
That endless vigil kept,
And through each brain on hands of pain
Another's terror crept.

Alas! it is a fearful thing
To feel another's guilt!
For, right within, the sword of Sin
Pierced to its poisoned hilt,
And as molten lead were the tears we shed
For the blood we had not spilt.

The Warders with their shoes of felt
Crept by each padlocked door,
And peeped and saw, with eyes of awe,
Grey figures on the floor,
And wondered why men knelt to pray
Who never prayed before.

All through the night we knelt and prayed,
    Mad mourners of a corpse!
The troubled plumes of midnight were
    The plumes upon a hearse:
And bitter wine upon a sponge
    Was the savior of Remorse.

The cock crew, the red cock crew,
    But never came the day:
And crooked shape of Terror crouched,
    In the corners where we lay:
And each evil sprite that walks by night
    Before us seemed to play.

They glided past, they glided fast,
    Like travelers through a mist:
They mocked the moon in a rigadoon
    Of delicate turn and twist,
And with formal pace and loathsome grace
    The phantoms kept their tryst.

With mop and mow, we saw them go,
    Slim shadows hand in hand:
About, about, in ghostly rout
    They trod a saraband:

And the damned grotesques made arabesques,
Like the wind upon the sand!

With the pirouettes of marionettes,
They tripped on pointed tread:
But with flutes of Fear they filled the ear,
As their grisly masque they led,
And loud they sang, and loud they sang,
For they sang to wake the dead.

"Oho!" they cried, "The world is wide,
But fettered limbs go lame!
And once, or twice, to throw the dice
Is a gentlemanly game,
But he does not win who plays with Sin
In the secret House of Shame."
No things of air these antics were
That frolicked with such glee:
To men whose lives were held in gyves,
And whose feet might not go free,
Ah! wounds of Christ! they were living things,
Most terrible to see.
Around, around, they waltzed and wound;
Some wheeled in smirking pairs:
With the mincing step of demirep

Some sidled up the stairs:
And with subtle sneer, and fawning leer,
Each helped us at our prayers.

The morning wind began to moan,
But still the night went on:
Through its giant loom the web of gloom
Crept till each thread was spun:
And, as we prayed, we grew afraid
Of the Justice of the Sun.

The moaning wind went wandering round
The weeping prison-wall:
Till like a wheel of turning-steel
We felt the minutes crawl:
O moaning wind! what had we done
To have such a seneschal?

At last I saw the shadowed bars
Like a lattice wrought in lead,
Move right across the whitewashed wall
That faced my three-plank bed,
And I knew that somewhere in the world
God's dreadful dawn was red.

At six o'clock we cleaned our cells,
At seven all was still,
But the sough and swing of a mighty wing
The prison seemed to fill,
For the Lord of Death with icy breath
Had entered in to kill.

He did not pass in purple pomp,
Nor ride a moon-white steed.
Three yards of cord and a sliding board
Are all the gallows' need:
So with rope of shame the Herald came
To do the secret deed.

We were as men who through a fen
Of filthy darkness grope:
We did not dare to breathe a prayer,
Or give our anguish scope:
Something was dead in each of us,
And what was dead was Hope.

For Man's grim Justice goes its way,
And will not swerve aside:
It slays the weak, it slays the strong,
It has a deadly stride:

With iron heel it slays the strong,
    The monstrous parricide!

We waited for the stroke of eight:
    Each tongue was thick with thirst:
For the stroke of eight is the stroke of Fate
    That makes a man accursed,
And Fate will use a running noose
    For the best man and the worst.

We had no other thing to do,
    Save to wait for the sign to come:
So, like things of stone in a valley lone,
    Quiet we sat and dumb:
But each man's heart beat thick and quick
    Like a madman on a drum!

With sudden shock the prison-clock
    Smote on the shivering air,
And from all the gaol[4] rose up a wail
    Of impotent despair,

---

4 The Reading Gaol was built in the 1800s and remained operational till 2013.

Like the sound that frightened marshes hear
From a leper in his lair.

And as one sees most fearful things
In the crystal of a dream,
We saw the greasy hempen rope
Hooked to the blackened beam,
And heard the prayer the hangman's snare
Strangled into a scream.

And all the woe that moved him so
That he gave that bitter cry,
And the wild regrets, and the bloody sweats,
None knew so well as I:
For he who live more lives than one
More deaths than one must die.

IV.

There is no chapel on the day
On which they hang a man:
The Chaplain's heart is far too sick,
Or his face is far to wan,
Or there is that written in his eyes
Which none should look upon.

So they kept us close till nigh on noon,
    And then they rang the bell,
And the Warders with their jingling keys
    Opened each listening cell,
And down the iron stair we tramped,
    Each from his separate Hell.

Out into God's sweet air we went,
    But not in wonted way,
For this man's face was white with fear,
    And that man's face was grey,
And I never saw sad men who looked
    So wistfully at the day.

I never saw sad men who looked
    With such a wistful eye
Upon that little tent of blue
    We prisoners called the sky,
And at every careless cloud that passed
    In happy freedom by.

But there were those amongst us all
    Who walked with downcast head,

And knew that, had each got his due,

They should have died instead:
He had but killed a thing that lived
Whilst they had killed the dead.

For he who sins a second time
Wakes a dead soul to pain,
And draws it from its spotted shroud,
And makes it bleed again,
And makes it bleed great gouts of blood
And makes it bleed in vain!

Like ape or clown, in monstrous garb
With crooked arrows starred,
Silently we went round and round
The slippery asphalte yard;
Silently we went round and round,
And no man spoke a word.

Silently we went round and round,
And through each hollow mind
The memory of dreadful things
Rushed like a dreadful wind,
An Horror stalked before each man,
And terror crept behind.

The Warders strutted up and down,
And kept their herd of brutes,
Their uniforms were spick and span,
And they wore their Sunday suits,
But we knew the work they had been at
By the quicklime on their boots.

For where a grave had opened wide,
There was no grave at all:
Only a stretch of mud and sand
By the hideous prison-wall,
And a little heap of burning lime,
That the man should have his pall.

For he has a pall, this wretched man,
Such as few men can claim:
Deep down below a prison-yard,
Naked for greater shame,
He lies, with fetters on each foot,
Wrapt in a sheet of flame!

And all the while the burning lime
Eats flesh and bone away,
It eats the brittle bone by night,
And the soft flesh by the day,

It eats the flesh and bones by turns,
    But it eats the heart alway.

For three long years they will not sow
    Or root or seedling there:
For three long years the unblessed spot
    Will sterile be and bare,
And look upon the wondering sky
    With unreproachful stare.

They think a murderer's heart would taint
    Each simple seed they sow.
It is not true! God's kindly earth
    Is kindlier than men know,
And the red rose would but blow more red,
    The white rose whiter blow.

Out of his mouth a red, red rose!
    Out of his heart a white!
For who can say by what strange way,
    Christ brings his will to light,
Since the barren staff the pilgrim bore
    Bloomed in the great Pope's sight?

But neither milk-white rose nor red
    May bloom in prison air;
The shard, the pebble, and the flint,
    Are what they give us there:
For flowers have been known to heal
    A common man's despair.

So never will wine-red rose or white,
    Petal by petal, fall
On that stretch of mud and sand that lies
    By the hideous prison-wall,
To tell the men who tramp the yard
    That God's Son died for all

Yet though the hideous prison-wall
    Still hems him round and round,
And a spirit may not walk by night
    That is with fetters bound,
And a spirit may but weep that lies
    In such unholy ground,

He is at peace—this wretched man—
    At peace, or will be soon:
There is no thing to make him mad,
    Nor does Terror walk at noon,

For the lampless Earth in which he lies
    Has neither Sun nor Moon.

They hanged him as a beast is hanged:
    They did not even toll
A requiem that might have brought
    Rest to his startled soul,
But hurriedly they took him out,
    And hid him in a hole.

They stripped him of his canvas clothes,
    And gave him to the flies;
They mocked the swollen purple throat
    And the stark and staring eyes:
And with laughter loud they heaped the shroud
    In which their convict lies.

The Chaplain would not kneel to pray
    By his dishonored grave:
Nor mark it with that blessed Cross
    That Christ for sinners gave,
Because the man was one of those
    Whom Christ came down to save.

Yet all is well; he has but passed
    To Life's appointed bourne:
And alien tears will fill for him
    Pity's long-broken urn,
For his mourner will be outcast men,
    And outcasts always mourn.

V.

I know not whether Laws be right,
    Or whether Laws be wrong;
All that we know who lie in gaol
    Is that the wall is strong;
And that each day is like a year,
    A year whose days are long.

But this I know, that every Law
    That men have made for Man,
Since first Man took his brother's life,
    And the sad world began,
But straws the wheat and saves the chaff
    With a most evil fan.

This too I know—and wise it were
    If each could know the same—

That every prison that men build
    Is built with bricks of shame,
And bound with bars lest Christ should see
    How men their brothers maim.

With bars they blur the gracious moon,
    And blind the goodly sun:
And they do well to hide their Hell,
    For in it things are done
That Son of God nor son of Man
    Ever should look upon!

The vilest deeds like poison weeds
    Bloom well in prison-air:
It is only what is good in Man
    That wastes and withers there:
Pale Anguish keeps the heavy gate,
    And the Warder[5] is Despair

---

5 Wilde here describes the Warder as despair itself. It is interesting to note that one of the warders at Reading Gaol had described him as a man of intellect, and his 'intellectual force' made him stand apart from the rest of the convicts. An article in *Bruno Weekly* of 22 January, 1916, revealed the thoughts of the warder in-charge during Wilde's imprisonment at Reading Gaol. The warders were aware that the punishment was 'terrible' and admitted that Wilde must also be suffering because of his 'sensitive temperament.'

For they starve the little frightened child
    Till it weeps both night and day:
And they scourge the weak, and flog the fool,
    And gibe the old and grey,
And some grow mad, and all grow bad,
    And none a word may say.

Each narrow cell in which we dwell
    Is a foul and dark latrine,
And the fetid breath of living Death
    Chokes up each grated screen,
And all, but Lust, is turned to dust
    In Humanity's machine.

The brackish water that we drink
    Creeps with a loathsome slime,
And the bitter bread they weigh in scales
    Is full of chalk and lime,
And Sleep will not lie down, but walks
    Wild-eyed and cries to Time.

But though lean Hunger and green Thirst
    Like asp with adder fight,
We have little care of prison fare,
    For what chills and kills outright

Is that every stone one lifts by day
    Becomes one's heart by night.

With midnight always in one's heart,
    And twilight in one's cell,
We turn the crank, or tear the rope,
    Each in his separate Hell,
And the silence is more awful far
    Than the sound of a brazen bell.

And never a human voice comes near
    To speak a gentle word:
And the eye that watches through the door
    Is pitiless and hard:
And by all forgot, we rot and rot,
    With soul and body marred.

And thus we rust Life's iron chain
    Degraded and alone:
And some men curse, and some men weep,
    And some men make no moan:
But God's eternal Laws are kind
    And break the heart of stone.

And every human heart that breaks,
    In prison-cell or yard,
Is as that broken box that gave
    Its treasure to the Lord,
And filled the unclean leper's house
    With the scent of costliest nard.

Ah! happy day they whose hearts can break
    And peace of pardon win!
How else may man make straight his plan
    And cleanse his soul from Sin?
How else but through a broken heart
    May Lord Christ enter in?

And he of the swollen purple throat.
    And the stark and staring eyes,
Waits for the holy hands that took
    The Thief to Paradise;
And a broken and a contrite heart
    The Lord will not despise.

The man in red who reads the Law
    Gave him three weeks of life,
Three little weeks in which to heal
    His soul of his soul's strife,

And cleanse from every blot of blood
    The hand that held the knife.

And with tears of blood he cleansed the hand,
    The hand that held the steel:
For only blood can wipe out blood,
    And only tears can heal:
And the crimson stain that was of Cain
    Became Christ's snow-white seal.

VI.

In Reading gaol by Reading town
    There is a pit of shame,
And in it lies a wretched man
    Eaten by teeth of flame,
In burning winding-sheet he lies,
    And his grave has got no name.

And there, till Christ call forth the dead,
    In silence let him lie:
No need to waste the foolish tear,
    Or heave the windy sigh:
The man had killed the thing he loved,
    And so he had to die.

And all men kill the thing they love,
    By all let this be heard,
Some do it with a bitter look,
    Some with a flattering word,
The coward does it with a kiss,
    The brave man with a sword!

Palanquin Bearers

by Sarojini Naidu
Published in
The Golden Threshold (1905)

[This poem is a beautiful depiction of a long-gone Indian tradition, where it was customary for men to carry the bride to her new home in a palki, a palanquin.]

Lightly, O lightly we bear her along,
She sways like a flower in the wind of our song;
She skims like a bird on the foam of a stream,
She floats like a laugh from the lips of a dream.
Gaily, O gaily we glide and we sing,
We bear her along like a pearl on a string.

Softly, O softly we bear her along,
She hangs like a star in the dew of our song;
She springs like a beam on the brow of the tide,
She falls like a tear from the eyes of a bride.
Lightly, O lightly we glide and we sing,
We bear her along like a pearl on a string.

If

by Rudyard Kipling

Published in

Rewards and Fairies (1910)

If you can keep your head when all about you
    Are losing theirs and blaming it on you,[1]
If you can trust yourself when all men doubt you,
    But make allowance for their doubting too;
If you can wait and not be tired by waiting,
    Or being lied about, don't deal in lies,
Or being hated, don't give way to hating,
    And yet don't look too good, nor talk too wise:

If you can dream—and not make dreams your master;
    If you can think—and not make thoughts your aim;
If you can meet with Triumph and Disaster
    And treat those two impostors just the same;
If you can bear to hear the truth you've spoken
    Twisted by knaves to make a trap for fools,
Or watch the things you gave your life to, broken,
    And stoop and build 'em up with worn-out tools:

---

1 The poem's inspiration was Kipling's friend, Dr. Leander Starr Jameson, introduced to Kipling by the Prime Minister of Cape Colony of southern Africa, Cecil Rhodes. This line is believed to commemorate his loyalty. Jameson had planned to raid Transvaal in order to overthrow the Boer Government. The raid was unsuccessful and Jameson was captured and imprisoned. Even then, Jameson didn't reveal the involvement of the British government in the raid.

If you can make one heap of all your winnings
    And risk it on one turn of pitch-and-toss,
And lose, and start again at your beginnings
    And never breathe a word about your loss;
If you can force your heart and nerve and sinew
    To serve your turn long after they are gone,
And so hold on when there is nothing in you
    Except the Will which says to them: 'Hold on!'

If you can talk with crowds and keep your virtue,
    Or walk with Kings—nor lose the common touch,
If neither foes nor loving friends can hurt you,
    If all men count with you, but none too much;
If you can fill the unforgiving minute
    With sixty seconds' worth of distance run,
Yours is the Earth and everything that's in it,
    And—which is more—you'll be a Man, my son!

Piano

by D H Lawrence

Published 1913

Softly, in the dusk, a woman is singing to me;
Taking me back down the vista of years, till I see
A child sitting under the piano, in the boom of the
tingling strings
And pressing the small, poised feet of a mother who
smiles as she sings.

In spite of myself, the insidious mastery of song
Betrays me back, till the heart of me weeps to belong
To the old Sunday evenings at home, with winter
outside
And hymns in the cosy parlour, the tinkling piano
our guide.

So now it is vain for the singer to burst into clamour
With the great black piano appassionato. The glamour
Of childish days is upon me, my manhood is cast
Down in the flood of remembrance, I weep like a
child for the past.

The Love Song of J. Alfred Prufrock

by T S Eliot

Published in *Poetry: A Magazine of Verse* (1915)

S'io credesse che mia risposta fosse
A persona che mai tornasse al mondo,
Questa fiamma staria senza piu scosse.
Ma percioche giammai di questo fondo
Non torno vivo alcun, s'i'odo il vero,
Senza tema d'infamia ti rispondo.

Let us go then, you and I,[1]
When the evening is spread out against the sky
Like a patient etherized upon a table;
Let us go, through certain half-deserted streets,
The muttering retreats
Of restless nights in one-night cheap hotels
And sawdust restaurants with oyster-shells:
Streets that follow like a tedious argument
Of insidious intent
To lead you to an overwhelming question . . .
Oh, do not ask, "What is it?"
Let us go and make our visit.

---

1 There is a single speaker in the poem—Prufrock—who, while narrating, reveals things about himself unintentionally. Thus, it can be called a dramatic monologue, and has sometimes been compared to Robert Browning's poems such as *My Last Duchess* and *Porphyria's Lover.*

In the room the women come and go
Talking of Michelangelo.

The yellow fog that rubs its back upon the
    window-panes,
The yellow smoke that rubs its muzzle on the
    window-panes,
Licked its tongue into the corners of the evening,
Lingered upon the pools that stand in drains,
Let fall upon its back the soot that falls from
    chimneys,
Slipped by the terrace, made a sudden leap,
And seeing that it was a soft October night,
Curled once about the house, and fell asleep.

And indeed there will be time[2]
For the yellow smoke that slides along the street,
more popular notion that time was never enough.
Rubbing its back upon the window-panes;
There will be time, there will be time

---

2 Modernist literature had defined a notion of time different from the chronological time. Time could be fluid, and not defined into set hours, minutes or seconds of the clock. In this poem, time appears to be at a standstill, almost frozen.

To prepare a face to meet the faces that you meet;
There will be time to murder and create,
And time for all the works and days of hands
That lift and drop a question on your plate;
Time for you and time for me,
And time yet for a hundred indecisions,
And for a hundred visions and revisions,
Before the taking of a toast and tea.[3]

In the room the women come and go
Talking of Michelangelo.[4]

And indeed there will be time
To wonder, "Do I dare?" and, "Do I dare?"
Time to turn back and descend the stair,
With a bald spot in the middle of my hair —
(They will say: "How his hair is growing thin!")

---

3 The poem is replete with the aspects of the works published during the modernist movement, with the characters often displaying an existential angst that the modern man of twentieth century felt. Here too, the speaker, Prufrock, is fed up of his life, and wants it to be about more than just 'tea' and 'cakes'.

4 This line is being repeated here to highlight the monotony of such social gatherings, where the women were having the same conversation as they did in the last gathering about the same artist.

My morning coat, my collar mounting firmly to the chin,
My necktie rich and modest, but asserted by a
simple pin —
(They will say: "But how his arms and legs are thin!")
Do I dare
Disturb the universe?
In a minute there is time
For decisions and revisions which a minute will
reverse.
For I have known them all already, known them all:

Have known the evenings, mornings, afternoons,
I have measured out my life with coffee spoons;
I know the voices dying with a dying fall
Beneath the music from a farther room.
So how should I presume?

And I have known the eyes already, known them all—
The eyes that fix you in a formulated phrase,
And when I am formulated, sprawling on a pin,
When I am pinned and wriggling on the wall,
Then how should I begin
To spit out all the butt-ends of my days and ways?
And how should I presume?

And I have known the arms already, known them all—
Arms that are braceleted and white and bare
(But in the lamplight, downed with light brown hair!)
Is it perfume from a dress
That makes me so digress?
Arms that lie along a table, or wrap about a shawl.
And should I then presume?
And how should I begin?
Shall I say, I have gone at dusk through narrow streets
And watched the smoke that rises from the pipes
Of lonely men in shirt-sleeves, leaning out of
windows? . . .

I should have been a pair of ragged claws
Scuttling across the floors of silent seas.

And the afternoon, the evening, sleeps so peacefully!
Smoothed by long fingers,
Asleep . . . tired . . . or it malingers,
Stretched on the floor, here beside you and me.
Should I, after tea and cakes and ices,
Have the strength to force the moment to its crisis?
But though I have wept and fasted, wept and prayed,
Though I have seen my head (grown slightly bald)
brought in upon a platter,

I am no prophet — and here's no great matter;
I have seen the moment of my greatness flicker,
And I have seen the eternal Footman hold my coat,
and snicker,
And in short, I was afraid.

And would it have been worth it, after all,
After the cups, the marmalade, the tea,
Among the porcelain, among some talk of you and me,
Would it have been worth while,
To have bitten off the matter with a smile,
To have squeezed the universe into a ball
To roll it towards some overwhelming question,
To say: "I am Lazarus, come from the dead,
Come back to tell you all, I shall tell you all"—
If one, settling a pillow by her head
 Should say: "That is not what I meant at all;
 That is not it, at all."

And would it have been worth it, after all,
Would it have been worth while,
After the sunsets and the dooryards and the
 sprinkled streets,
After the novels, after the teacups, after the skirts that
 trail along the floor—

And this, and so much more?—
It is impossible to say just what I mean!
But as if a magic lantern threw the nerves in patterns
on a screen:
Would it have been worth while
If one, settling a pillow or throwing off a shawl,
And turning toward the window, should say:
"That is not it at all,
That is not what I meant, at all."

No! I am not Prince Hamlet, nor was meant to be;
Am an attendant lord, one that will do
To swell a progress, start a scene or two,
Advise the prince; no doubt, an easy tool,
Deferential, glad to be of use,
Politic, cautious, and meticulous;
Full of high sentence, but a bit obtuse;
At times, indeed, almost ridiculous—
Almost, at times, the Fool.

I grow old . . . I grow old . . .
I shall wear the bottoms of my trousers rolled.

Shall I part my hair behind? Do I dare to eat a
peach?

I shall wear white flannel trousers, and walk upon
the beach.
I have heard the mermaids singing, each to each.

I do not think that they will sing to me.

I have seen them riding seaward on the waves
Combing the white hair of the waves blown back
When the wind blows the water white and black.
We have lingered in the chambers of the sea
By sea-girls wreathed with seaweed red and brown
Till human voices wake us, and we drown.

The Soldier

by Rupert Brooke

Published 1915

[The Treaty of London had declared Belgium an independent kingdom and signified its neutrality. It had been signed by the Allied Forces and Germany. However, Germany crossed Belgium's borders to invade France in August 1914. Britain then declared war on Germany since it had violated this Treaty. Also, Britain had to protect itself. Germany controlling Belgium posed a danger to them since Belgium's ports were close to the British coasts.

Brooke wrote this poem a year into the First World War, evocating patriotism for England. In this poem, the speaker unflinchingly declares that he would consider it an honour to die for his country.]

If I should die, think only this of me:
    That there's some corner of a foreign field
That is for ever England. There shall be
    In that rich earth a richer dust concealed;
A dust whom England bore, shaped, made aware,
    Gave, once, her flowers to love, her ways to roam;
A body of England's, breathing English air,
    Washed by the rivers, blest by suns of home.

And think, this heart, all evil shed away,
    A pulse in the eternal mind, no less

Gives somewhere back the thoughts by
England given;
Her sights and sounds; dreams happy as her day;
And laughter, learnt of friends; and gentleness,
In hearts at peace, under an English heaven.

The Road Not Taken

by Robert Frost

Published in

Mountain Interval (1916)

Two roads diverged in a yellow wood,
And sorry I could not travel both[1]
And be one traveler, long I stood
And looked down one as far as I could
To where it bent in the undergrowth;

Then took the other, as just as fair,
And having perhaps the better claim,
Because it was grassy and wanted wear;
Though as for that the passing there
Had worn them really about the same,

And both that morning equally lay
In leaves no step had trodden black.
Oh, I kept the first for another day!
Yet knowing how way leads on to way,
I doubted if I should ever come back.

I shall be telling this with a sigh
Somewhere ages and ages hence:

---

1 While walking with Frost, his friend, Edward Thomas would often express regret on not traversing a different path. This everyday act was then transformed into a poem.

Two roads diverged in a wood, and I—
I took the one less travelled by,[2]
And that has made all the difference.

2 Though it is not exactly clear what Frost meant by this, the common interpretation has come out to be that Frost is talking about his career choice here. He decided to be a poet, a profession not opted for by many. But in choosing to be a poet, he has earned himself a name.

Dulce Et Decorum Est

by Wilfred Owen

Published 1920

Bent double, like old beggars under sacks,
Knock-kneed, coughing like hags, we cursed
    through sludge,
Till on the haunting flares we turned our backs,
And towards our[1] distant rest began to trudge.
Men marched asleep. Many had lost their boots,
But limped on, blood-shod. All went lame; all blind;
Drunk with fatigue; deaf even to the hoots
Of gas-shells dropping softly behind.

Gas! GAS! Quick, boys!—An ecstasy of fumbling
Fitting the clumsy helmets just in time,
But someone still was yelling out and stumbling
And flound'ring like a man in fire or lime.—
Dim through the misty panes and thick green light,
As under a green sea, I saw him drowning.

In all my dreams before my helpless sight,
He plunges at me, guttering, choking, drowning.

If in some smothering dreams, you too could pace
Behind the wagon that we flung him in,

---

1 The description of this battlefield is from Wilfred Owen's personal experience from fighting in the trenches of France in World War I.

And watch the white eyes writhing in his face,
His hanging face, like a devil's sick of sin;
If you could hear, at every jolt, the blood
Come gargling from the froth-corrupted lungs,
Obscene as cancer, bitter as the cud
Of vile, incurable sores on innocent tongues,—
My friend, you would not tell with such high zest
To children ardent for some desperate glory,
The old Lie: *Dulce et decorum est*
Pro patria mori.[2]

---

2 The last line translates to 'It is sweet and honourable to die for one's country.' The poem seems to be countering Jessie Pope's *War Poems* that were a call for the young men to enlist in fighting in the war, claiming that those who did not, were cowards who wouldn't volunteer when their country desperately needed them.

The Red Wheelbarrow

by William Carlos Williams

Published in

Spring and All (1923)

So much depends
upon

a red wheel
barrow

glazed with rain
water

beside the white
chickens.

Stopping by Woods on a Snowy Evening

by Robert Frost

Published in

New Hampshire (1923)

Whose woods these are I think I know.
His house is in the village though;
He will not see me stopping here
To watch his woods fill up with snow.

My little horse must think it queer
To stop without a farmhouse near
Between the woods and frozen lake
The darkest evening of the year.

He gives his harness bells a shake
To ask if there is some mistake.
The only other sound's the sweep
Of easy wind and downy flake.

The woods are lovely, dark and deep,
But I have promises to keep,
And miles to go before I sleep,
And miles to go before I sleep.